To, Sam

25th March '15

Janak Mistry

All glory comes from daring to Begin

JOURNEY IN TIME WITH TIMELESS MEMORIES

Janak Mistry

A motorcycle tour to untouched Himalayan regions

www.windsor-verlag.com

© 2014 Janak Mistry
All rights reserved.

Publisher: Windsor Verlag
ISBN: 978-1-627840-74-3

Cover Design: Julia Evseeva
Photos: Janak Mistry
Layout: Julia Evseeva

No part of this publication may be reproduced, distributed, or transmitted in any form or by any means, including photocopying, recording, or other electronic or mechanical methods, without the prior written permission of the publisher, except in the case of brief quotations embodied in critical reviews and certain other noncommercial uses permitted by copyright law. For permission requests, write to the publisher.

INDEX

Acknowledgment	7
Chapter 1 PLANNING THE JOURNEY TO THE HEAVEN AND BACK	9
Chapter 2 ZIP ZAPPING THE LUGGAGE	18
Chapter 3 THE JOURNEY TO THE HEAVEN BEGINS	22
Chapter 4 INTO THE WILDERNESS	27
Chapter 5 TO THE LAND OF GOMPAS	33
Chapter 6 PARADISE OF INDIA	42
Chapter 7 SPLASHED IN THE INDUS	48
Chapter 8 MEANDERING OUT AND ABOUT LEH	55
Chapter 9 CONNECTING TO THE DIVINITY	66
Chapter 10 LADAKH SAND DUNES & VISITING THE LORD	72
Chapter 11 BACK TO WHERE WE STARTED FROM	84
Chapter 12 THE LONGEST DAY OF MY LIFE	90
FAQs	101
Bibliography	105
About the Author	107

ACKNOWLEDGMENT

It is never easy to follow a dream until it comes true and never too easy to share the experience when you are through. It is never about following the book or the rules but make one of your own and following it religiously. With every difficulty while planning and making this trip happen, I would like to thank the almighty who had bestowed me with enough strength, will and courage to face the roughest and the toughest terrains with grandeur. I would also like to thank Royal Enfield for their indigenous machine, which helped me make my dream come true with an ease and a Thump I would never forget.

A vote of thank you and a bow down goes to my family who believed in me and blessed me with everything they can. It is because of them I have broadened my horizon and think beyond imagination, always. I would surely want to continue that and make it better in the years to come.

I would also like to thank my friend Dhrumit for the crazy, noble and wacky idea he had. I would not be able to do this without you buddy.

A big vote of thanks to Rohit for his larger than life experience and helping me plan the trip. It would not have been possible without your words of encouragement and planning.

I would also like to thank Hemant, Mitesh, Ravi, Suresh, Sumit, Hardik and Kunal for their constant support and encouragement during the trip. It means a lot to me.

Thank you Arpit, Tanvi, Mansi, Kartik, Pratiksha and Kunwar Yatin in guiding me through the unknown and helping me expand my horizon and reach new possibilities. It wouldn't have moved a step further without your constant support and encouragement.

A Big Thank You to some of my friends around Europe who with their beautiful pictures encouraged me on clicking the essentials of any trip I make. It would not have been possible without all of you to make this very piece of work so vibrant and lively.

To Fernando, who encouraged me and pushed me to write this very piece of work.

To all those adults who shared the same dream, to the youths who have the same dream and to the children that will have the same dream.

Chapter 1

PLANNING THE JOURNEY TO THE HEAVEN AND BACK

It all started as a joke between friends who always end up coming to a thin line of conversation about the next holiday destination and accidently it was the beautiful and scintillating Leh-Ladakh this time. Besides the beautiful destination, a revelation was the mode of transport we would use while travelling all the way out there a motorcycle. It was a jaw-dropping idea but I did manage myself well and took the idea sportingly. While I was busy working in a different city I receive a casual call from my friend about this very trip. The voice on the other end sounded more than excited than what he was I guess. It was not easy for me to decide for it required a good amount of funds for the entire trip and I do not earn that very handsome amount which I can shell out in a single go.

It was not easy to decide for I was unaware of what I would be going through in this very holiday trip. However, I had saved up some money to buy myself a new smart phone. I still was not convinced with the idea about travelling to Leh-Ladakh and that to on a motorcycle. Besides a good amount of money, it would also be essential to have that courage and vigour to go for a long ride. Somewhere deep down I was not too sure or may be not even fit to go ahead with this plan. The excitement, I could hear about the trip whenever I called up my friends enticed me towards this very trip and made it more than irresistible to go ahead and think about it.

With an approaching weekend, I decided to invest the whole of weekend researching about the place and everything about it. It was after that very day I did think a lot about the plan but never had the courage to discuss or open up in front of anyone. I was more than scared listening about the plan for this trip than anyone else because of the many crashes I have had in the past and if at all, something goes wrong I would not want to live a damaged life. Upon researching, it was even scarier than I thought about which had put me in a Dilemma. It was after a good researching and reading from many travellers who have done this very trip I plan to give it a second thought. While reading from various bloggers it was one particular blogger who had narrated everything about the various trips she had done on her motorcycle though not in India but on some of the best roads in the world. She is in her 50s. After reading her blog, it was more than clear about her hunger to ride more and to some of the less travelled destinations in the world. It was not easy digesting this very fact that a lady in her 50s can ride in various parts of the world which when compared to me who is half her age can surely give a thought about it. She did it solo and without any fellow riders I would be riding solo but with my friends around me to help me out.

It was a tough decision to make especially after reading about that woman. Though I am not an egoistic person I still had that feel of an under-achiever specifically after what I read and saw on the internet about Leh-Ladakh.

Planning a motorcycle trip sounds cool but stepping in without planning is planning for failure and welcoming fatal outcome. Keeping this very idea in mind I prepared my body in a way, which would help me, keep fit in the cold weather and at the same time be strong enough to handle, maneuver and ride my motorcycle with enough strength and confidence.

I would have to be ready for the best and worst of the weather conditions, as I would be riding for a good 4500 kilometres of a round trip. Besides strengthening the immune system, it is necessary to have the right riding gears, which fits well and comfortable to wear for a long time. Riding your motorcycle with half or no riding gears would be welcoming death with both hands.

Everyone likes enjoying the vacation but when it comes to preparing for the so-called vacation, it sounds a bit too awkward and offbeat. I had the similar thought before I could actually understand the intensity of the journey I would be doing and the mode of transport I would be using. I considered various factors before I started preparing myself for the trip.

- Weather conditions
- Distance to be covered
- Number of days I take to prepare myself

WEATHER CONDITIONS

Going up to the northern most point in India to the Himalayas is no easy task especially because of the weather conditions. Though the weather in the month of July would be pleasant, it is prerequisite to be prepared for the worst of the scenarios. The temperature was at a good average of 25-30 degrees during the day and dipped to 4-5 degrees in the night. It all depends on where you stay. In the location between Manali and Leh, it would be lower than 5 degrees with a bit of heavy winds at times. Leh is pleasant in the month of July with a good 30 plus degrees in the afternoon. It is necessary to drink lots of water and fluids to avoid dehydration. As the location is high above the sea level, it is necessary to protect the skin from the UV rays, as they are more powerful than what we have at the sea levels. There is a common notion to have some rum or vodka in the cold weather but it surely is not advisable on the high altitude. Since you need to breathe more to compensate for low oxygen at high altitudes, drinking could make it more to experience "Hypoxia"- a pathological condition in which the body as a whole or a region of the body is deprived of oxygen supply (Leibenluft, 2008).

DISTANCE TO BE COVERED

Covering a good 4500 kilometres of a distance is no easy feat and preparing yourself mentally is the key step in preparing for the journey. Many times people do go ahead with this kind of thrilling plan but do back out in the last moment or half way through as it becomes unbearable to ride and maintain the fatigue level. It is necessary to have an experience to ride for a minimum of three hundred kilometres to have a good idea about the ride fatigue and your personal ability to handle the motorcycle for a long time thereby being vigilant at all times. I did a couple of short riding trips to various cities from Mumbai which gave me a fair idea about what charges I would have to do to prepare my body and how can I better the art of riding long distances. It is important to understand your body and the pain areas after those short trips. It would not only give you a clear picture about the areas you need to work on but also improve your riding posture which might be one of the reason which adds up to your ride fatigue.

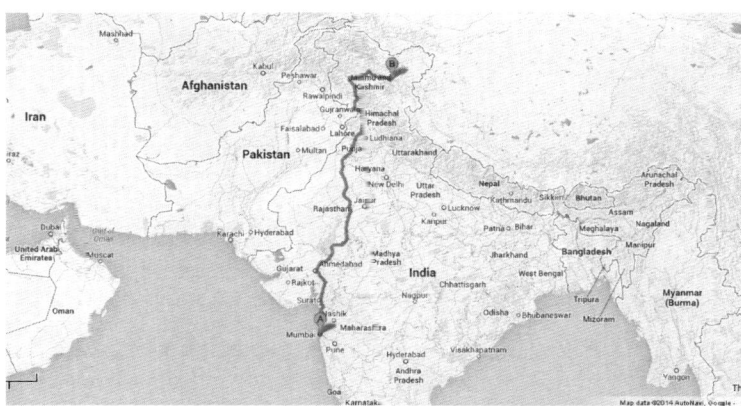

**Route map for the entire planned trip
(Source: googlemaps.com)**

13

Our body and the motorcycle react differently in different terrains and weather conditions. I luckily had a chance to ride on different terrains and weather conditions, which gave me a good idea on what would various weather demand from a long distance rider. Monsoon in India is from the month of June to September, which means I need to acclimatise with riding in the rains. However, it does not rain heavily after Manali but you never know what is in store. It is always better to be prepared for the best and the worst.

NUMBER OF DAYS I WOULD TAKE TO BE PREPARED

It was the third week of March and the plan to leave for this vey trip was in the month of July. I had just about enough time to save up some more money and start training if at all I make up my mind to go for the trip. As I have had some of the severe injuries in the past. I consulted my physiotherapist about this very trip and asked him about how good were my chances to go ahead and be successful in doing this very trip to which he just replied "if you are not planning, you are planning for failure" followed by a good go-ahead kind of a smile on his face. It gave me a good level of confidence but the worst is yet to come as I need to be in good shape mentally and physically in order to go ahead with this trip smoothly.

Before I go ahead and give my final nod to my friends, I gave it a good thought about the severity of the trip and my level of preparation with the time I had to be prepared. With enough time to be in shape and save up some money, I gave my friend the final nod about the trip. It was time now to change my routine, diet and sleeping pattern to begin with.

Before I planned my workout I gave myself a few days wherein I adjust my body clock in a way which would not only help me in the days to come but also give me a good rest after an excruciating workout I would have to go through.

Because of the tight financial condition and not enough time to join the gym, it was best that I start my workout at home and prepare myself. With no trainer around and no big mirrors for motivation, it was tough to get started. I stopped working out after I had my first crash in 2008 and resuming something I loved felt great but was not as open and as flexible, I am now as I was back then. It was necessary to bring back the confidence and get back in shape.

I started running for a good one month. I started with running for two kilometres, which I later increased to a good five kilometres. The best part about doing a workout is the feeling of liveliness I had during the day. It did give me a good level of self-confidence and made my willpower strong. Besides a good result in my log, it was important that I felt good about what I do and how I do it. It not only gave me a good boost in my energy level but also made me more disciplined than what I was. With a good control on my diet, I could see the results in my body and the progress that I always wanted. In this slow but steady process, I realised that working out, maintaining your body is quintessential, and if you fail to do it would surely fail to keep you energised and charged. Days turned into weeks and I could see a different me in the mirror. It surely was happening well, I could feel that every day, and with every single breath, I took.

Keeping yourself fit is essential when it comes to riding for a long distance. Though the entire body goes through a lot of strain it is your lower back, wrist, shoulders, arms and ankles, which play a key role in keeping you happy for a long time while riding. I began with maintaining a healthy diet and a routine, which would help me develop my body in the desired form. Consuming Less carbohydrates and fats was the key step to start followed by a good exercise regime. An exercise focusing on lower back is essential as it helps you maintain the posture and eliminate the pain after you finish riding for the day.

Though the lower back helps in maintaining the correct riding posture it is necessary to work out on your thighs and the core body in order to have a better control while on low speed.

It is important to have a strong wrist and overall palm for it would be used to control and maneuver the motorcycle well. A weak palm or wrist is the first point to ride fatigue, which is not a good sign. It is important to strengthen your fingers for it would be very much you would have to do while riding on hills, boulders and while crossing the streams.

It was time now to move on from a general workout pattern to a more specific workout plan which would help me focus on my posture and breathing pattern. Once the body gains the stability and endurance with the exercises for your lower back, legs, wrists and fingers it is important to work a bit harder on your arms. It is important to have strong arms in order to have a stable and fatigue free ride and maneuverability while on bad roads. Besides making it easy to control the motorcycle, they do add a lot of confidence while riding and add a good shape and tone to your overall physique.

Maintaining a healthy diet and regular exercising regime, would not only help you boost the confidence but make you feel better and prepare yourself mentally for the trip. It took me a good three months to maintain the routine and be physically fit. These three months do include a twenty-one days of no sugar, no salt, and no fast food diet. The idea behind eliminating excessive sugar and salt is to maintain the sugar level in your body and providing enough room for quality and nutritious food. It is mandatory to resume eliminated food diet before you commence your journey to avoid excessive sugar intake while on the journey and prepare your body to any kind of food intake as that would be the case while on the trip. Your body is your biggest weapon in a place with limited assistance and less oxygen.

Chapter 2

ZIP ZAPPING THE LUGGAGE

While preparing for this kind of a trip it is essential to pack your luggage in a way which makes it lighter thereby giving you enough room to add every essential item you would need while on the run. Because of the nature of the trip is important to carry fewer clothes.

Besides keeping the luggage as light as possible, it would also be better to have a different bag, which carries the day-to-day essentials. This would not only disturb your principal bag and at the same time becomes more convenient accessing the day-to-day items.

Many people ride using the tank bag, which is a convenient option to keep your documents, camera, maps and some high-energy snack. It is convenient because of its accessibility and an even option to distribute the access weight you wish to distribute from your principal baggage or your quick access baggage. It is essential to avoid keeping any sharp objects in the tank bag to avoid any injuries and or a huge cut in the bag. Riding with equally distributed weights is the key to safe and smooth riding. To keep the luggage intact and avoid making more of the movements it is advisable to use bungee nets instead of the bungee cords, for nets can cover the whole luggage.

Covering the luggage with a tarpaulin sheets not only provides a good safety from the rains but also can be handy to cover your motorcycle after you finish riding for the day. Tarps do come handy if at all your bag falls away from each other (60kph.com, 2006).

However, we had a car along with us, which made it a lot easier for me to ride without luggage but it does call for tactful packing. It is best to avoid taking something straight from the shelf for it would not be as comfortable as compared to those, which you have used before. During the last few days before the departure, I did use all my riding gears while riding. This not only gave me a good feel about all of it but also made me a bit acquainted.

My baggage consisted of
- **Riding Helmet** – a good and comfortable riding helmet is necessary. It is always better to carry some wet wipes along to clean up the helmet visor after every ride to avoid any scratches and get a clear view.
- **Riding Jacket** – Because of the variations in the weather conditions, it is essential to carry a riding jacket which is water resistant and has multiple pockets to keep the essentials while in an emergency.
- **Riding Gloves** – A regular city riding gloves would not suffice because of the extremely cold and breezy morning it is necessary to carry an extra pair of riding gloves, meant for winter riding.
- **Balaclava** – It is necessary to wear a balaclava under a helmet for various reasons. Because you would be riding for the whole day it is natural to sweat because of which the helmet might start stinking with all the sweat being absorbed in the pads and cushions inside thereby making it uncomfortable to wear. Because of the rough, dusty and windy terrain, a good balaclava would not only keep your face fresh after the ride but also save you from those chilly winds especially in the morning. Besides the protection, it is easier to wash thereby giving you a fresh feel every time you wear it.

- **Riding boots** – a good comfortable and used pair of riding boots can always be a first choice. It is better to carry the used and old riding boots and let them get in to the muddy slush than the new pairs. Besides being spoilt, it is always comfortable to wear used pair of boots than the new ones, which takes a lot of time being comfortable in to.
- **First aid Kit** – it is necessary to a carry a good well-equipped and updated first aid kit along with the required medicines than to repent on something during the urgent need of the hour. It is always better to show it to your family doctor before you leave.
- **Tool kit** – essential tools can save up a lot of time especially on those rough terrains. It is always better to carry an extra pair of spanners, screwdrivers and some of the multi-utility tools, which can get the ride back on the run at least until the mechanic shop.
- **Extra spares**- an extra pair of tyre tube, bulbs, spark plugs, brake pads and tube valves does come handy. If they are unused in the trip, they can always be used later when your motorcycle needs a repair.
- **Wet suite** (Raincoat) – It would not be safe riding in the rains but it is always essential to wear them specially when it is drizzling and it is manageable to ride at least until the nearby village or a shelter. Besides saving the rider from the rains, they do give good warmth and do not let the winds enter your body. It is always better to carry a bright colour wet suit, which is easier to spot at from a long distance.
- **Woollen wear** – It is better to carry some woollen wear along to avoid being a victim to bad weather.
- **Thermal Inners** – it is essential to have a couple of thermal wear along with you to avoid the cold breeze on the high altitude.
- **Sunscreen lotion** – Due to the high altitude location it is necessary to cover the body whenever possible otherwise it is always better to apply sunscreen lotion

before you go out in the sun. Because of the strong sun rays the skin when exposed to sun for a longer time would burn and peal of in no time.
- **Toiletries** – it is better to carry only the essentials you require in the toiletries. Carrying an extra bottle of lotion or a perfume would not be a good idea for every extra item in the luggage counts.
- **Clothing** – carrying a few t-shirts and a pair of sturdy jeans and that should suffice. However, it is always better to carry an extra pair of jeans just in case you need it.

Lighter the luggage easier to handle!

Chapter 3

THE JOURNEY TO THE HEAVEN BEGINS

It was great planning and preparing for the trip but it was not as easy as it sounded for everyone who had planned this in the first place. It was not pleasant knowing about this but well that was the fact. After a delay for a good two weeks, we were finally on for the trip. To say I was excited would be more of an understatement. After all those days went by and people walking out of the plan, it was not easy to digest the fact that we were finally on the track.

The excitement and enthusiasm to see the mountains and enjoy the ride was beyond imagination. Nevertheless, to reach that very point it was a long journey with a good amount of rest in order to be ready for the treacherous ride.

We were finally off from my hometown called "Bilimora"- a small town famous for some of the most unusual things but above all kind-hearted people. It felt great seeing the goodbyes and good lucks with a warm smile from the near and loved ones. However, the initial plan was to ride from my hometown, which was now to driving up till Manali and than riding from there on. With an addition of two more wheels in the journey, it felt a bit easier and comfortable than what we would have gone through if at all we would have rode from the beginning.

As we left and touched the highway, it was no stopping until we managed to cover some distance but to our hard luck, there seemed some problem in one of the rear tyres. We had no choice but to halt at a fuel station where we noticed that the one of the rear tyre had a crack. It was big enough to blow the tyre on a high speed. There was no option but to change it as soon as we can. Being a Sunday it was a bit difficult to find any tyre shop open though it was not difficult to find one after a bit of looking around. By the time, we showed the tyre to the shopkeeper the crack was already a bit bigger than what it was initially. He advised us to change both the rear tyres as that will make them even and give us a better grip especially in the terrain we would be driving to. He did a quick job and we were back on track but now with already a lot of time gone by, we had to rush a bit so that we can cover a good distance before dusk. Luckily, with no rains on the way it was easy cutting the distance.

While everyone back home was excited about the trip, some were not happy. Though it felt bad, it would not be right to not enjoy the trip, show them the best through captured videos and pictures, and make them believe that they were very much a part of this trip too.

As it was the first day and everyone was more than enigmatic about the whole experience it was time now that everyone was keen on planning about what to do when we reach Manali and before we start riding. As I have not been to Manali before I so wish to see the beautiful place and try different delicacies for I have heard so much about it through my friends Though the plan sounded well it was not what everyone wanted to go ahead with. Their plan was to reach Manali as soon as we can and check out the motorcycles and leave the next day for a ride to Leh. I was not a bit keen about this plan for it was not something, which everyone does not to go around in the city and have a good time but to acclimatize the body to higher altitude. This not only makes it easier to ride further but also make it less complicated for people who have breathing problems on high altitude. I never gave much thought about it for it was too early to think about it right now.

It was time now that my phone beeped with a message saying that we have entered the state of "Rajasthan" a neighbouring state to Gujarat. It felt great to be in a different state especially when you are driving down. I had never done this before and felt good about it. It was already late evening by now which I realised about when my stomach started growling. The next stop soon had to be for our dinner but it had to wait for we were close to reaching the city of Udaipur where we can have various options for food and surely some place where we can hit the brakes and doze off.

As I saw the milestone numbering ninety-two for Udaipur I could see, the rain drops splashing on my screen. It was not a good idea to drive in the rains but we had no choice for we were in the middle of nowhere and not too far from the city of Udaipur. I was slow but steady and did manage to combat the rains and reach Udaipur. The city was new to my friends and me. We had no choice but to decide our dinner location based on an outlook of the restaurant. After a good wandering around, we did manage to find a good place. It was Shraddha Restaurant, which looked more of a place known for its Rajasthani delicacies. We wasted no time and called for Dal Baati churma one of the famous delicacy in Rajasthan and a must try if you are in Rajasthan.

Dal Baati churma is famous because of various reasons. Besides the nutritional value, it also has a longer shelf life, higher nutritional value and requires minimal quantity of water for its preparation. Daal is prepared from lentils and can be a bit spicy at times. Baati is prepared from grilled or baked wheat balls, which relished with churma, traditionally cooked with coarsely ground wheat and cooked in ghee and sugar. Traditional way to enjoy the delicacy is to crush the Baati, pour some ghee over it, and relish it with Daal followed by some churma. Besides the amazing taste, it is high in nutritional value and less expensive to cook which makes it one of the most favourable delicacies offered during various celebrations (rajdhani.co.in, n.d.).

Having the traditional food of Rajasthan was a great experience and did pep all of us up besides make it a bit heavier than we actually thought about. The next big question after having such a sumptuous meal was surely not to hit the bed but hit the road and cover up whatever distance we could before we plan to go to bed. Everyone was fine with that, to which we are on the road again now to reach our next destination-the Pink city of Jaipur. It was a good four hundred and eighteen kilometres of a drive. With smooth road and a talkative company, reaching the pink city should not be a problem. I was on the navigator seat now enjoying the road. It was after a good four hours of a drive we reached Jaipur. It was 2 am in the morning and everyone looked super tired. With a small hotel we had halted at, we wasted no time and got our rooms and crash with a plan to leave no earlier to 7 am in the morning.

It feels different to be in a different city in a different province. Though it is a part of the same country, it has so many different things that I have not seen so far in the cities I have lived in during my education. The change in approach and their hospitality is so very different from what I had experienced before. I guess this is what a foreign tourist experiences while in India and visiting different cities. It felt special not being in a different place but exploring the unexplored in the way I always wanted to.

Distance Covered
Kilometres clocked: 1,139

Route map (Source: googlemaps.com)

Chapter 4

INTO THE WILDERNESS

Get excited and enthusiastic about your own dream. This excitement is like a forest fire - you can smell it, taste it, and see it from a mile away (Waitley, n.d). The excitement and adrenaline rush was clearly seen on my face. With the planning and re-planning for the entire route it was finally the day we start riding. However, before we move forward I looked and checked up everything once again to be more than sure about everything was up to the mark. As we fired up the engine, it felt great and super energetic. With the hour hand touching twelve and making a strike at 6 am in the morning, it was time to move on the epic journey.

It felt great leaving Manali and riding close to the river Bias enjoying the changing beauty of the Mother Nature. It was now time that we started climbing up the hill It was not easy initially to adjust on a different motorcycle specially when you are used to riding a good 900 cc Harley Davidson which now switched to a mere 350 cc Royal Enfield makes a lot of difference. It was beyond complaining and more of enjoying the beauty and the ride until something unusual happened to my motorcycle. With a few jerky moves, it came to a halt on a slope. I had to pull up on the side and see what the problem could be in the meanwhile my fellow riders did come back and helped me check on where the problem could be. It becomes a bit difficult and annoying to some extent when something similar happens in the very beginning of your journey. Though it is a big turn off, I did take it as a lucky timing for what if my motorcycle made a halt right in the middle of a muddy slush. It would not be as easy as it is now. Finally, after a good inspection in all the possible areas we did notice that the battery wire was off from the main screw and had to be re-fitted. With a few screwdriver moves, it was back on track and my motorcycle was back to life. The incident was a revelation and a quick learning lesson on being patient in situations like this. Though this was small, we have to be ready for worse that is yet to come.

It feels great to ride on a hilly terrain but with that very enjoyment, it is necessary to be more than sharp and vigilant at all times. While riding up the Rohtang Pass it felt great but within no time, we were in a huge traffic cue and in between the knee-high mud slush. It was not easy riding through that muddy slush and manoeuvring through the stranded traffic. It took a lot of patience, courage and riding skills to go ahead. I was stuck many times in the mud but with the help of the fellow riders and army officers on duty I could get out of the muddy slush and managed to ride forward. For anyone who wishes to ride to Leh has to pass through this treacherous, muddy and one of the most challenging roads. While riding forward I did meet many people who were stuck for hours and some already turning their motorcycles back to Manali for they doubted if they would be able to make it to the summit and ride further. This gave me a good idea about how one has to be mentally strong and stable thereby focusing on every move. It definitely was not easy for us to reach the summit but felt great passing the summit and moving forward towards our next stop, which was at a small village called Kaylong. Besides being a small village, it also serves as a good known spot for riders to make a halt. Riding again after a brief halt it felt great and energetic specially after clearing the mud slush at the Rohtang pass.

With open road and rising altitude, it was very much clear with the way our motorcycle started performing. I could feel the deteriorating power in the motorcycle, which made me shift the gear more often. I had no choice but to keep the pace until the road was good and broad enough.

The well-surfaced roads turned into old patchy roads, which slowly introduced us to a gravel road. It was very much clear about the kind of roads we would have to face further to reach our overnight halt destination at zingzing-bar. With a good narrowing roads and changing weather we decided to stop over at a check post in a village called Darcha. A small village with some amazing tent restaurants and welcoming people we decided to sit in one of the places and have some of the best momo's with some extra spicy chilly pickle. While we left from Manali it was around 10 degree Celsius and the time when we made the halt it was more than 25 degrees Celsius. While riding in this kind of a weather and terrain it is necessary to be hydrate and consume a lot of water. This not only helps you with the oxygen requirements in the brain but also helps you in being sharp and agile at all times.

The road between Manali to Leh is famous for its raw heat that can not only make you sick but also dehydrate your body to an extent, which leads you to a blackout in vision. Being aware of this very scenario, I did drink a lot of water and kept my sugar levels high having some of the confectionaries handy in my pocket at all times.

While riding on those isolated roads we crossed an Indian Army camp where an officer was waiting to get a lift from someone who was going towards Leh. I was more than happy to help the officer. It was a smooth journey until we came across another stream where he asked me to stop by as he could get down and cross the stream on foot and help me cross it on my motorcycle while guiding me on the best possible patch to ride on.

With a swift start again on ride, it was time now to cross some of the ice-cold streams. It was not easy crossing the first stream but when I saw a fellow rider crossing from the other end it looked a bit easier. With a slow movement on my clutch I did move ahead to cross the stream. Focused more on the stones and some of the huge potholes I did manage well to cross it and ride ahead. Though the stream was not that deep, as it seemed to be and did not have that kind of a force there is a chance we might have some of the fast flowing streams ahead. While in this region, it is necessary to cross the streams either early in the morning or in the evening after 4 pm to avoid high water level and excessive flow. I did have this very concept in my mind but when it comes to practically crossing a stream in front of you, it is not feasible to look at the watch and water in the stream to slow down.

Thinking about this very concept and I could see and hear a stream which was a bit bigger and a bit rougher than the previous one. I could see a truck crossing it and felt it more of a walk in the park but it was way stronger and longer than what I had assumed. With a bit of a confidence crossing the previous stream I used all my focus and physical energy to balance the motorcycle while it jumped from some of the rocks underneath and did manage to cross it well. With a sigh of relief, I moved forward this time even more ready for anything, which comes my way.

Picture 1: Riders struggling on the Rohtang pass.
Picture 2: The ride in the mud slush can do a lot to you than just giving YOU a fresh patch of mud.
Picture 3: Momo's with chilly pickle at Darcha.
Picture 4: The first stream that I crossed.
Picture 5: Our overnight halt at Zingzingbar.
Picture 6: Besides comfortable and warm blankets, the tent had everything to keep us warm and comfortable.

After a short while, I had to see off the officer and ride forward to Zingzingbar. Finally, after a good one hour of ride we managed to reach the village and felt shocked to see that it was not a village but a small flat land with a few tents, which served as a kitchen, restaurant and a place where you can sleep during the night.

After riding for a good fourteen hours, it was not possible to ride further. Everyone got in the tent and relaxed while the woman who owned the tent was more than co-operative in providing us with whatever we needed.

While relaxing in the warm tent I did think about the life of all those who stay here and do their daily business which is just for three months in a year. The life out here is not easy for it has less oxygen, windy evenings and extremely cold night. With nearly no energy left to move even an inch we discussed about the route for the next day while having dinner and that was it.

Distance Covered
Kilometres Clocked: 171

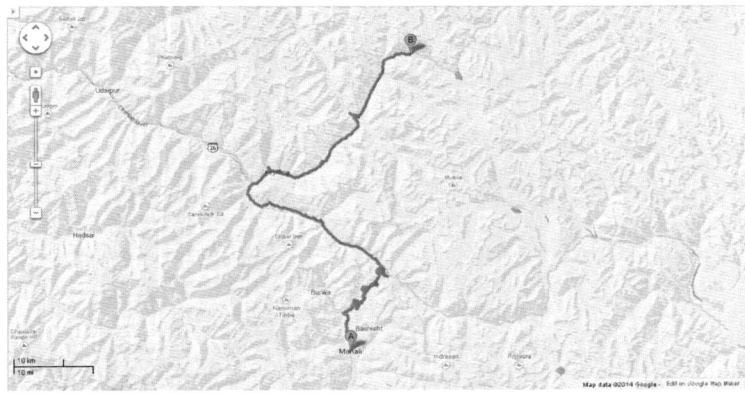

Route map (Source: googlemaps.com)

Chapter 5

TO THE LAND OF GOMPAS

The ride from Manali to Zingzingbar was a bit exhaustive, a little adventurous, a bit more than exciting, and above all a bit more than painful but with a good sound sleep and much needed rest, it was time now to ride again. It was 4:00 am in the morning and according to the rough calculation if we start riding soon, we should be able to reach Leh before dusk.

However, we felt fresh and ready it was not easy to drag the motorcycle on the road and fire up the engine. Besides the cold winds and a temperature of a good 3 - 4 degree Celsius, it was not easy to start riding again. Hot and tasty Ginger, Lemon & Honey tea kept me more than warm for a while and while I started riding it was not more than ten minutes when my hands started freezing because of the regular riding gears. I had no choice but to keep my palm movement aggressive and keep them agile as we could not afford to freeze and loosen up for the road ahead was more treacherous and time consuming. With my hand barely moveable, my visor kept having a fog every time I exhale. It was tough to ride with the closed visor and super cold to open it up to avoid the fog. I had no choice but to open up the air vents on top of my helmet, which would help me avoid the fog thereby making it a bit easier for me to ride. It was comfortable for a while but started getting worst when we could see the sun.

Besides the fog on the helmet visor, it was the sunrays, which not only made me blind but also made it more than irritating to ride in the similar fashion. I had no choice but to keep all the vents open and open up the visor to have a clear vision. It felt chilly for a while but made it worst to ride in this fashion for I had teary eyes because of the cold winds. The vision problem kept me on toes for a good two hours. I did have a pair of sunglasses but could not wear them in the helmet because of the balaclava it would make it very uncomfortable, as I am not used to wearing sunglasses inside the helmet. After riding for a good six hours, we had crossed a mere eighty kilometres. I guess this leaves you with the imagination about the kind of roads we were riding on or I can say a patch of similar heighted rocks and boulders. By now, I already had a bad backache. The road definitely tested my patience and endurance to the core. It was not the physical but the mental strength, which does the job in this very terrain. The road we were riding on had no trees, no river flowing by and definitely no humanity around besides some of the riders passing by. By now, the temperature was more than warm which made me more than thirsty.

Picture 1: With practically no roads to ride on it became more than difficult to ride.
Picture 2: The only bridge in the world, which has to be set first and then rode on.
Picture 3: The only living creature I could see while on a particular stretch without trees. I wonder how they survive.
Picture 4: Tents at Pang village.
Picture 5: With few varieties to serve, they make the best they can.
Picture 6: Ooh these shoes. They looked different when I started.
Picture 7: No mean look but an actual tired face.

I had to make do with the confectionaries in my pocket and keep my mind occupied in some or the other thoughts. There are times when I went blank and could not think of anything. With every pass we climbed, it was more of an anticipation to see the humanity and normalcy around and in that very anticipation I saw a bridge, which I had to cross by to ride, further but could not do that so easily. As it is in a rough and rugged terrain, it is necessary that you check and settle the plates before you ride on them. It was not possible to move those plates single-handedly, which made me wait for my fellow riders who wear nearing the bridge. After a good team effort, we could cross the bridge and ride on.

With the rise in temperature and different shades of brown hills passing by I could spot some wild deers on the hills far away. Trying to get a better look at them and enjoy the view I could not see them well because of the camouflaged colours they had with the hills it became more than difficult seeing them for long. I could not resist clicking the closest possible shot. After a good forty-eight kilometres from that very spot, I entered a village called Pang. Though being a village, it had a few tents here and there, which offered the bedding and food options. I stopped by at one of the biggest tents around and entered the place asking for some time to rest before I could place any order for food. In the meanwhile, my fellow riders came in too and laid their achy back on the well-set bedding. No one said a word for a good half an hour. Everyone looked more than tired, exhausted and a bit disturbed passing by from the very no creature zone without roads. It was not easy for any of us to digest the fact that we managed to cross that very rough patch.

After a good one hour, the little girl who seemed to be the daughter to the owner of the very tent asked my friend if we would like to have something for lunch. Due to excessive heat and exhaustive ride no one was in the mood to eat anything but to keep the body strong and hydrated, it was essential to eat well and drink enough water as we were already at a good 15,000 ft above the sea level and would have a good elevation further on. Collecting all my energy and endurance, I asked for a soupy red kidney beans and a bowl of rice with Ginger, Lemon and Honey tea. Consuming more of the citric acid helps prevent throat infection, caused due to excessive dust, and changing weather. It felt better after a good healthy meal. It was a time now to move on but it was not easy to gear up again and start riding. It was not possible to get up without a strong will and determination to reach the summit. However, before we could start riding again we had to fuel up the motorcycles to avoid unforeseen halt.

With a goodbye wave to the tent owner, I was again on the roll and ready to ride on further. The road was no different after Pang too and we had to keep the patience to move slow but steady in motion. This time the road started getting narrower than before. I recall an incident when I saw an Indian Army truck coming from the opposite direction and to let it pass by I had no choice but to lean my motorcycle on the hill and be on a side letting the truck pass by. It was only after the truck had passed by I had to pick up my motorcycle and start riding again. It is important to keep an eye on the top of the hill and see who is coming from the other end besides seeing the vehicles in the front. Being vigilant about the moment from the vehicles in the front not only gives a brief idea about the road conditions but caution you on a particular juncture, which needs more attention.

I had managed to pass by a good fifteen kilometres, which is when I could see the fresh road. It feels good to ride on a road I was riding on after a long time.

With a constant increase in the height above sea level, it was not easy to breathe and lack of responsiveness from the motorcycle made things a bit difficult. It was after a while of riding we pass by a board, which mentioned that we were on the second highest motorable point in the world the Bara-Lacha La pass at a good 16,043 ft above sea level. It felt great to be on one of the highest motorable roads in the world. After a brief halt for some pictures it was back to riding and with a good clean, open road it felt good to ride without any jumps and bumps but that smooth feel did not last long for my motorcycle made an unfriendly gesture and stop responding to the throttle. It feels more than irritating when your motorcycle do not perform when you are on an open road and not very far from the destination.

While inspecting every possible area many riders passed by but no one stopped. It was after a while two of the riders stopped by and came to us asking if everything was ok. This was not only surprising but a bit shocking too for no one before him had stopped and asked me something like this. After a brief conversation and his quick effort to find where the problem was he mentioned that he is a mechanic and works with the same company from where we had rented our motorcycles. I would not call this a coincidence but a pure luck.

Picture 1:   The amazing soupy Red Kidney Beans with Rice.
Picture 2:   Enjoying the best I can at low speed.
Picture 3:   An open road to the end of the horizon.
Picture 4:   The Baralacha La pass-Second Highest Motorahle point in the world.
Picture 5:   The mechanics who helped me fixed more than my motorcycle.
Picture 6:   It felt great getting closer to the destination.
Picture 7:   The beautiful Ladakh Gate.

With all his efficiency and skills, he managed to get my motorcycle back to life. I had no words to thank him and did ask him about how much I had to pay him. Looking at my monetary approach, he smiled and said, "Do enjoy your time and come back safe. We will surely meet before you go back home". I could not say anything but gave him a smile and a firm handshake.

Being a part of the monetary and materialistic world I never knew when my approach had changed from being a simplistic to a money-oriented approach. The incident taught me a lesson about humanitarian approach and its value. It was not easy digesting the fact that I would have never done anything like that for free. Monetary value is not everything. Your point of view matters.

After riding for a good fourteen hours, I was delighted to see the milestones with double- digit kilometres to the destination. It felt great but because of the excessive body ache and absolutely no energy for excitement, I kept on riding smooth.

Clocking some of the last few kilometres to the destinations was tough to clock due to ride fatigue but I am proud to say I made it and made it first. The main gate called the "Ladakh Gate" which marks the entry to the city of Leh looked more than beautiful. With a big smile on my face, I was delighted and could not resist but stand before the gate and feel the change and enjoy the moment. It felt great talking to my parents after a good two days and narrating the whole incident about the road so far and the very gate I was in front of while talking to them. After a good ride, I could not wait to find a room in a guesthouse, take a hot shower and sleep.

While I had reached early, my friends and fellow riders were still on the way. I had no choice but to wait for them. After a good two hours of wait, we were good to enter the city and find ourselves a good place to stay. It was more than frustrating about the fact that we were not able to find any vacant rooms so far. With all the tiredness and riding all day long it was not easy being polite to the receptionists in different hotels I asked for the rooms. Finally after a good search we managed to find a hotel which was close the city centre and very much in between the lively shops. After a good negotiation on the price, we could park the motorcycles, enjoy the much-needed shower, and sound sleep.

It was no less than an achievement being in Leh after a long treacherous, breath taking and one of the most dangerous ride of my life but all said and done I was happy to see my face in the mirror which just said "you made it and made it well".

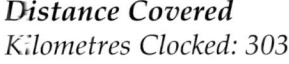

Distance Covered
Kilometres Clocked: 303

Route map (Source: googlemaps.com)

Chapter 6

PARADISE OF INDIA

With an alarm, buzzing up at 7 am in the morning it was good to be up but was not the right time to get up. I had a good sleep but I need much more of it to enjoy the day here in the city of Leh. It felt different and simply charismatic of whatever I could see out of the window. I was back to sleep and was not up until it was super hot around 2:00pm in the afternoon. I was shivering in the morning and now I was sweating heavily with a good thick duvet on my body. I was finally up and surprised to see that my friends and fellow riders were up already and enjoying some of the sumptuous snacks. The city looks beautiful and felt so different and not very much like in India for a change. I could not wait to get ready and explore the city but I preferred being in the bed and rest as much as possible as the fun and adventure is about to begin from this very city.

It feels great to connect to the world again and let them know about my whereabouts. However, it was great to disconnect from the world for a good two days. The silence and peace you get from being disconnected is priceless. It surely was not easy but it was not bad either provided you know the place and the changing weather. I preferred keeping my cell phone on a silent mode and not spoil the beautiful climate and feeling I was into with those annoying phone calls.

With all the fun and enjoyment I was into, I did experience that I was not able to speak in the same pace I was to. I had a bit of trouble breathing and had a mild headache. I did not experience something like this before. I ignored it initially thinking it might be from the exhausting journey and the schedule since last two days but it was not great going around with this condition, which is when I asked my friends about if they felt the same way I was experiencing. I was surprised to know that they were in the same position as I was in to. With a bit of a thought on what could the problem be I fetched some bottles of water from the nearby store. While climbing stairs I was not able to climb them easily as I was able to back home after some time. It felt as if I was climbing up the hill. It was not acceptable to my mind and heart about what I was going through for I have always been physically fit and have worked more than average specially to make this trip as smoother as possible by being strong mentally and physically.

I felt like I was being a man of a thousand questions but not even a single answer to them. It disturbed me for I was not feeling fit. All I could think of was to take a short nap thinking it might solve the problem and it did in a way. While I was sleeping the room service person was on the door unaware that he had knocked on the wrong door I looked at him. He was panting as if he had just finished a hundred metre dash and come down straight to my door. Upon asking him about if he was ok, he replied with a smile "it is because of the terrain and less oxygen everyone has this issue". This did answer some of my questions and realise what I could do to avoid this very problem. I wasted no time and had as much water as I can in regular intervals. I did have a few chocolates, which would give me a bit of energy. Instead of going back to sleep I chose to be awake and watch some television which would help divert my mind.

It was after a good two hours I could feel the change and it felt better to walk around and my head was ache free. It is important to acclimatise on a high altitude region, which can make you comfortable.

It was not until evening when I felt better and the best way to feel better would be to go around the city and divert my mind. It felt great seeing this very small city filled with so many tourists from around the world. The climate by now was pleasant as well, which was much-needed after what we all had been through for a good two days of extensively varying climate.

While going around in the city and visiting some of the shops I did notice that there were more females who worked and run a daily business compared to man. It was a bit different from a regular scenario in different parts of India I have visited so far. It felt great to see the women's power increasing and being at par with the male gender. While going around in the city we did manage to visit a mechanic where I had to get my motorcycle checked and make necessary repairs to avoid any further breakdowns. In the meanwhile my friends took our car to the service station for the general check up to avoid any further problems.

Picture 1: It is not a monument but an auditorium hall
Picture 2: The Thikse Monastery.
Picture 3: A prayer wheel at one of the junctions leading to the main market.
Picture 4: One of the main streets in the city of Leh.
Picture 5: Old Tibetan refugee market.
Picture 6: One of the coolest restaurant walls I have ever seen.
Picture 7: Though the streets are narrow, it does have broad-minded people.

While getting my motorcycle serviced I happen to speak to the mechanic about the experience, which we had since last two days. He seemed cool listening to the experience. He did share some of his experiences as well and that shocked me to the core. It was no less than jaw dropping to lend an ear to some of those horrifying incidences.

While talking about various tourist spots around the city of Leh he did mention that we would have to obtain an "Inner Line Permit". A permit to be obtained from a government office which would have some of the key details like the number of days you plan to visit, different locations you plan to visit, and members who plan to ride on their motorcycles mentioned on the permit with necessary initials of the officers in charge. It would not be possible to go without a permit, as it is a very sensitive area. I wasted no time and got our permits for the next seven days.

With everything ready, it was time now to eat something good and proper for dinner. Though I was hungry, I could not eat properly maybe because of the altitude sickness and maybe because of the exhaustive evening. I could not help but have a bar of chocolate, went straight to the room, and take a good rest.

My friends were busy enjoying the sumptuous dinner and talked about it while I was watching the television. It was after a good one hour one of my friend breaks the news about the plan for the next day. He had planned and booked up rafting for all of us. Rafting in the Indus River is one of a kind and the longest in India. Though I was excited, I was not sure of what to do. It was not that I was scared to go rafting but more on the lines for the distance to be covered. I did have a good endurance and strength but when we talk about rafting it is different because of the heavy flow, it is not easy. I said nothing and left everything on what the next day had for me.

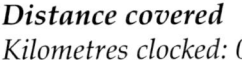

Distance covered
Kilometres clocked: 0

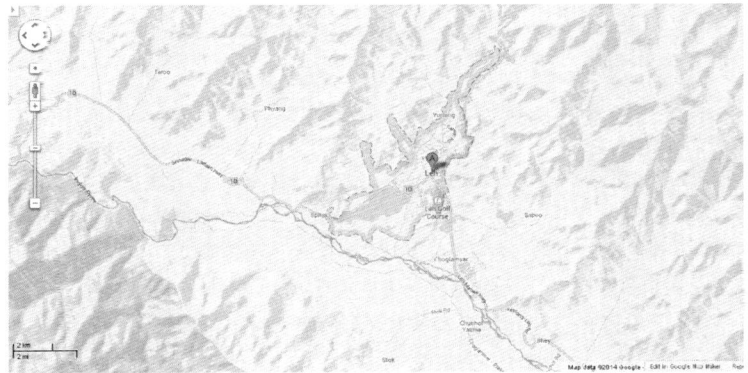

Route map (Source: googlemaps.com)

Chapter 7

SPLASHED IN THE INDUS

It is the day to get adventurous in the water. I was up early and ready to go for rafting. Though I have done rafting before this was a bit different because of the distance and the location and I was excited to go for it. With all ready for the adventure, we waited eagerly for the pick-up vehicle to arrive and pick us up. While sharing the experience about rafting with my friends we had our pick-up van, which already had three females from Korea who were joining us for rafting. While introducing ourselves initially and then the experiencing level in rafting it was just me who had a little experience whereas others were a novice. With all the eagerness and excitement I was flooded with various questions about what, how and when of the rafting. I did answer the best I could with whatever I knew and had experienced before. While on our journey, it was great interacting with the driver and got to know about various things about the city and the village where we are off for rafting.

While we arrived at the village, I was surprised to see just a few houses and a restaurant, which seemed all of it in the village. I wonder how people survive just in the middle of nowhere and far from the city of Leh. While I was admiring the beauty of that very small village, I did meet some more people who had come down for rafting. They had come all the way from Australia to try this very adrenaline rushing activity. It was great interacting with them and finally getting ready for the ultimate adventure. Though I have rafted before I did not get a chance to wear the wet suit for the distance to be covered was less and it was not as difficult as this one would be. Listening to this I already had shivers. I initially had the wet suit and than a windcheater kind of a jacket on top of it to avoid cold breeze affecting us when we get wet.

After getting ready, it was a time for a quick briefing session on how to react in worst of the situations. It was essential to be more than attentive for it can save my life. The instructor and the captain were more than easy on us but strict when it comes to following the rules. Finally, it was time to go. I was more than confident until the first rapid current which I strongly faced but when I had the second one I had a black out and loud, deep splash. The next thing I see when I open my eyes was the clear blue sky and my body shivering because of the cold water and difficulty in breathing because of the gushing water around me. I was in the water and flowed way ahead of where our raft was. It was the moment I would never forget all my life It was after sometime that I had the rescue kayak next to me. With every Do's and Dont's in my head I did exactly as told and held on to the loop on the kayak. It was after a few seconds I felt better and in no time I was next to the raft. The fellow rafters back in the raft pulled me on. Phew, it was a great sign of relief but a great adrenaline rush I could ever have. It was an out of the world experience.

Everyone looked at me and eased out only after I gave them a smile and a nod saying I was OK. It brought the cheers and smile to their tensed faces but it was in my head and heart about the experience I had. I went at the back and was barely able to pedal. It was all great until the time we had a stopover for a rest after fifteen kilometers. After a good stretching and rest, we left again and as per the captain and the coach, what we went through was nothing compared to what we are to see.

I was OK as I had seen the worst possible for which I was prepared mentally.

During the first current it was all good but a bit hard to control the body and the raft but on the second rapid current SPLASH! Two of the people sitting in the front are no more in the raft and not seen anywhere in the water. Everyone panicked shouting names and seeing around but could not see anything until a blue helmet floated in the water. Unknown to the fact that if my friend would still be under the helmet or it was just the helmet we moved forward and did notice that it was him in person. We went forward and rescued him. It was time now to SEARCH for the other person. He was way ahead than we had thought off. The rescue kayak did a great job and brought him to the raft. He weighs more than a hundred kilos, which means dragging him back was no less than a mission. Everyone in the raft was there to help him get on when we noticed that there was one more rapid current and if we do not balance the raft it would take all of us down. Holding him tight and using all the strength, I managed to pull him with my fellow rafters in while we had that rapid current. It was pure luck as we passed through that very rapid current in no time. It was crazy and very much on the edge but I am proud to say that we did it well.

Picture 1: Everyone looks happy and cheerful.
Picture 2: Ready for a splash.
Picture 3: The Do's and Dont's of Rafting. I guess this is what saved my life.
Picture 4: Off I go, ready to get splashed.
Picture 5: Cheerful and ready for a wavy ride.
Picture 6: The memorable spot where I was in the water.
Picture 7: Meters away physically and miles away mentally.

After the amazing rafting, it was time now to dry curselves and have the sumptuous lunch arranged by the organisers. After being in the water and travelling for such a long time, everyone was more than hungry and tired.

It felt great having a good simple lunch in a place so peaceful. I would not mind staying there for the whole day. It was time now to go back to the hotel and take the much-needed rest. It felt great until the time we took the lunch but it was more than tiring once we hit the road and on our way back to the hotel. Besides the hot weather in the afternoon, it was not easy being up during the journey. To keep myself up and enjoy the road I decided to chat with the driver and get to know a few things about some of the less known destinations we would be passing by. One such destination was the less known but truly magnificent 'Magnetic Hill'. Besides the magnificent view the hill had it also had the magnetic properties strong enough to pull the cars uphill. It was truly magical and mesmerising. Moving ahead of the Magnetic hill it was time now to see a Gurudwara Pathar Sahib.

Picture 1: Though a strong look on my face there was a shiver inside from the high-octane experience I had a while back.
Picture 2: The kayaker who saved my life, Hats off to his skills and courage.
Picture 3: Rescue operation for the two members who fell off the raft. I am the one who looks completely stretched in the raft ...
Picture 4: ... and the rescuing continues.
Picture 5: Paddling any more was a challenge in itself.
Picture 6: Glad to have made it and made it well.
Picture 7: I call that a Rafting effect. That is what happens after you do 30 kilometres of rafting and travel back.

However, we could stop by to make a visit and pay respect to the lord but because of the heavy duty rafting and the international co-passengers we had with us we decided to drive down to the Gurudwara the next day.

After a good short nap I had, we finally reached the guesthouse bidding good-bye to the females and the driver. The only agenda was now to go to the room and sleep like a baby. It was a great time and adventure we all had. It was time now to take rest and plan up the next day.

Distance covered
Kilometres clocked: 55.9

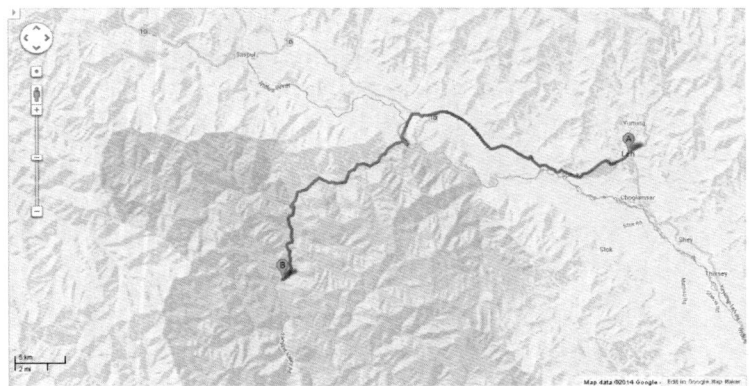

Route map (Source: googlemaps.com)

Chapter 8

MEANDERING OUT AND ABOUT LEH

The best part about having an adventurous day is to expect more in the days to come. It was not an easy experience for me rafting in the Indus River but it sure was one of the most memorable event of my life. After a good splashy rafting, it was plan now to head to the famous Pangong Tso Lake. They say 'if you have the right climate, it is one of the most beautiful lakes you would ever see'. Besides the beautiful view that the lake has it was interesting to know that more than sixty-five percent of the lake is in China and the rest falls in India. Listening to this very fact it was tough not to imagine about the view of that sixty percent of the lake, which is in China.

As the day rises with the dawn, it was time to ride again. However, the ride is not that far it sure sounded more than exciting to enjoy the ride and see the beautiful lake. With every possible scenario running in my head while having a shower it all came to a screeching halt when I heard the rain. It was the moment which made me blank and very much adamant to avoid riding in this very weather. A bit of drizzle would have been fine but with what I have been seeing made it more than sure that I would not be riding if the weather continues to behave in this very fashion. I could see my friends re-thinking about the plan too but it was only when they could see the rains slow down they resumed their preparation and moved on with the plan and convincing me to ride with them. With some of the worst experiences, I have had in the past while riding in the rains was more than enough to stop me. I was not worried about my riding gear but about the cold weather, I would have to pass through. I guess I was not prepared enough to take a chance with riding in the rains.

After a lot of convincing from my friends to join them for the lake, I was adamant on my decision. It was not a happy moment for them and for me but I guess one needs to be practical and selfish at times. It was finally a goodbye from my end and off they go with a roar in that very drizzling, cold and windy climate.

I was finally all alone in the guesthouse with nothing to do or take care off. I was blank for a good two hours and could not think of anything to do in this beautiful city. It was not that I was scared to go around and have a good time but it surely did not struck me or maybe I was more than resistant to step out in rains. It was not until the owner of the guesthouse came out of his office and asked me how I was and about my friends whereabouts I realised that if they are having a good time why shouldn't I. While in the general conversation about the life and times out here in this city it did struck me that if I have a free day why not utilise that very time and go around the city exploring and meeting new people.

With the general information I had from the research I did previously and some from the owner of the guesthouse it was more than enough to keep me going for a day and enjoy the time. The next thing I did was to pack my bag with enough water, woollen wear and some dried fruits just in case I needed some extra energy and I was off to explore. While leaving for the excursion the owner was more than happy to provide me with the city map and the places I can go and visit. It was no less than an icing on the cake.

While walking around in the city and enjoying my own time I never bothered to look at my cell phone but enjoyed more of the market and clicking pictures while finding the way to 'Shanti Stupa'. Shanti stupa is a white domed stupa or a chorten on a hilltop in chanspa. Besides the religious significance, the stupa is also famous because of the location, which provides one of the best panoramic views of the city of Leh (gurujigyomyo.com, 2013).

Reaching chanspa and seeing the stairs up to the stupa I went cold feet for it looked no easy with the steepness it had. I still decided to give it a go and off I was to climbing them one by one. It was after a mere fifteen steps I realised that I was not able to breathe properly. I had no choice but to take a halt after every fifteen steps I climbed. I enjoyed the view while my breath settled. After a good one hour of climbing, I reached Shanti stupa café, which made me more than hungry but eating, was for later for I had to visit the stupa and enjoy the view. By now, I was more than exhausted and out of my breath. With everything what I have been experiencing I still managed to move on. There was some force driving me forward and pushed me towards the stupa. It was unbelievable until I reached the Stupa and admired the beauty and peace. The structure of the Stupa looked magnificent and so appealing. Enjoying the beauty and purity of the very place was beyond imagination and far from something artificial. Going around the stupa and enjoying the view from different sides, it felt great and while exploring the location I did see a meditation room. It looked great from the inside. I could not resist but to go in and explore the beautiful interior. I always felt silence but after being in the meditation room and enjoying the peace, I could proudly say I could hear the silence.

While I sat there with my eyes open I could see a glimpse of my childhood, my good and some of the best days and things that I did come across. Everything came up like a fast forward movie in my head. I could not experience something like this before and it sure was not easy too.

My next stop was to enjoy some Ginger, Lemon & Honey Tea and a bowl of noodles at the Shanti Stupa café. It was more than simple and yet looked so special. I was more than happy to interact with the main chef out there and know the secret behind making one of the best Ginger Lemon & Honey Tea. I was never into drinking tea or coffee but I guess this was so different and so refreshing.

My next mission was to walk down the hill from those steep stairs and walk towards Leh Palace. While walking down the stairs I met a boy who was with a few of his friends who had come down from Switzerland and approached me to click their pictures. Seeing some of that shots I got myself clicked in addition, which led to a striking conversation about the cameras initially and then to the professional lives which is when I knew that he stays and works in Switzerland. I could not resist but ask him the obvious question about which place was better and what would you choose if you had a choice to choose one of them? Upon which he replied, "Switzerland is great and has always been my dream destination but Leh is special. If you need peace and a wish to discover yourself Leh is the place where I come to".

Picture 1: The majestic Pangong Tso Lake.
Picture 2: The Shanti Stupa.
Picture 3: At the Meditation room next to Shanti Stupa.
Picture 4: Noodles and Ginger Lemon & Honey Tea at the Shanti Stupa cafe.
Picture 5: Meeting the fellow traveller from Switzerland.
Picture 6: The lanes which leads to the Leh Palace.

I could not relate much to that, as it was barely a few days that I have been in Leh. While my next destination was the Leh Palace, they did give me a company until a good half way and guided me on the way further after which we were on our ways to different destinations. The best part about this journey is not the way they shape up but the way you end up meeting so many people from different parts of the world and different lifestyles. I believe it is one of the best ways to broaden your horizon and enjoy the moment while being with your own self.

While on my way to the Leh Palace, the route started to be a bit different, odd and a bit confusing too. However, the road was a short cut to the Leh Palace it was not easy going through some of the narrowest lanes and finding my way up the hill to the palace gates. It was after a good one and half hours of a walk through the houses, narrow lanes and some of the oldest buildings I could see the palace clearly. It looked great and bigger than what I had thought about in my mind. With some of the final steep steps and boulders, I did manage to reach the plain roads towards the Palace gates. It looked beautiful and so very different from the palaces I have visited before. Though the structure did not look Royal, it was no less beautiful and unique in its own way. With a big gulp of the water I walked up the stairs and notice that there is not enough light. It was a bit dark and very much self- explanatory with directions, posters, paintings and writings stuck on the walls. I had my own time reading everything I could.

Visiting every possible room and lobbies, I come across a Gompa or a palace temple. It looked so beautiful and so different from the inside. However, the temple was a bit dark and so very different from the Hindu temples it was a different experience seeing the goddess and some of the oldest Tibetan inscriptions wrapped in red silk cloth. As I was all alone in that very peaceful temple, I chose to come out soon. It was not scary but felt a bit strange. Maybe I was not too comfortable. While sitting on one of the benches in an open veranda I sipped on some water and enjoyed the panoramic view of the city and the mountains. It felt great being solo and not to convince, talk or ask about anything to anyone. I have always wanted this and I am glad I have had the time when I could be myself and not think about anything else.

After a much-needed rest on the bench, I was off to Tsemo Gompa Monastery. The king Tashi Namgyal built the monastery in 1430 AD as a mark of Buddhism (travel.india.com, 2013). Besides the panoramic view of the Zanskar range on one side and the beautiful city on the other it is a necessary visit. The route to the monastery was no easy as it was on the neighbouring hill. It was afternoon when I started climbing the hill. It was hot with scorching heat, which would make you cover your skin to avoid sunburns and heat stroke. With the slow but steady climb on the hill, I did manage to reach the summit after a good one hour. It was exhaustive especially because of the hot weather. Taking up a place in shade, I had to take up some rest and cool down to enjoy the beautiful monastery and the view it offered. This has been the third location of the day that I had reached now and every location gave an amazing panoramic shot of the beautiful city of Leh but none of them looked the same. The city looked so different from every angle.

It was different to enter the monastery and see the huge Lord Buddha idol. The walls covered in different paintings of Lord Buddha and his teachings and it smelt great. It felt good being inside and enjoying the paintings on the wall and worship the lord. After a good rest for some time, I was on my way back to the city. It was evening when I started walking down the hill.

It was exhaustive to walk down the narrow trek road, which leads to various locations. I was scared about not choosing the wrong lane and that is what happened when I saw a dead end in between the houses. It is frustrating to walk all the way up and then re- route your steps I had no choice but to do that. After reaching the city, it was time now to buy some fresh apricots and something to munch on for I have no energy to walk back to the city centre for my dinner. I was completely exhausted by the time I reached my guesthouse. Looking at me the owner of the guesthouse asked me about where all I had been to upon which when I narrated the story. Listening to what I had done for the entire day, he was awestruck knowing the fact that I did everything on the foot. He wasted no time, rushed to the kitchen, and fetched some water and some sweets. I was surprised seeing what he had offered me. I had no choice but to accept that and continue sharing my experience.

After sitting for a good one hour, I still did not have enough energy to walk towards my room that was on a good third floor. I chose to be on the reception and surf the internet while resting my legs on the chair. It was after some time that one of the fellow guests came over on the reception and wished to surf the internet on her tablet. She tried asking one of the porters around for the password to access the wireless internet but could not get the desired information.

Picture 1: The magnificent Leh Palace.
Picture 2: At the Leh Palace entrance.
Picture 3: Inside the Palace temple.
Picture 4: At the Tsemo Gompa Monastery.
Picture 5: At the Tsemo Gompa Monastery.
Picture 6: Prayer flags at the Tsemo Gompa Monastery.
Picture 7: The Vegetarian Thukpa.

After a while, I hear a sweet voice, which asked me if I knew the password to the wireless internet. I was more than willing to help her out with the password and get it going on her tablet. It was after a while we happen to strike a conversation after which it was no looking into my cell phone screen. We talked about everything from the motorcycles to the city and the experiences in our own cities. It was great to have a healthy interaction to someone you are unknown to especially in an unknown city. It was after a while her friend joined the conversation followed by her mother. I finally had a great company to have a healthy conversation. After sharing my experiences so far on the trip, they were enthralled with what we had been through so far.

It sounded more than challenging to them and I guess it would be for anyone who has never experienced riding on such a treacherous terrain. I finally took their leave on my way to the room where I thought of having the fruits and watching some television. They wished to have some traditional delicacies but unknown to the city they did ask me about any places I was aware of. I did manage to name a few restaurants, which were close by, and I had been to with my friends to which they did ask me to join them. I was not too sure but after a lot of convincing and persuasion, I joined them. While on the way to the restaurant, we did talk about many things but rushed up on the restaurant, as everyone was more than hungry. After ordering the sumptuous and soupy Thukpa a traditional Tibetan dish adopted from the Chinese soupy noodles. The relishing bowl of soupy noodles is available in both vegetarian and non-vegetarian options (chicken. ca, 2012). I did share some of my experiences during the day and I am happy to say they loved it. After enjoying the sumptuous meal, we were on our way back to the hotel where I could not wait to hit the bed.

It was a pleasant experience meeting some unknown people and share some of the similar experiences. It felt great for a change to talk to someone I do not know and interact beyond any boundaries.

Distance covered
Kilometres clocked 12.5 kms

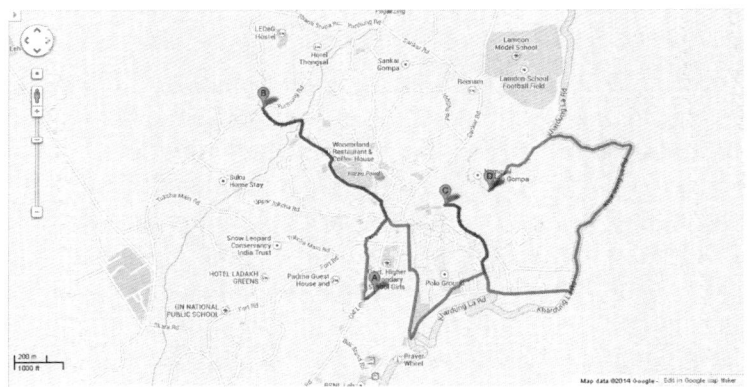

Route map (Source: googlemaps.com)

A to B - Guesthouse to Shanti Stupa
B to C- Shanti Stupa to Leh Palace
C to D – Leh Palace to Tsemo Gompa Monastery

Chapter 9

CONNECTING TO THE DIVINITY

Seeing the unseen and doing the unplanned was, the order of the day yesterday but I had another free day in my hand with absolutely nothing at all planned. It felt great being relaxed and free in the peaceful place with no one to talk to and hear on. These mornings are special and I so enjoyed it thinking about so many things. It is difficult to enjoy such mornings in the city life where the world is in a hustle bustle and though you are still it is always the distraction, which kills you mentally. After a good relaxing morning, it was time to decide on what are the spots I am yet to cover and make the best of the free day. After a bit of a research looking at the map, which I had from the owner of the guesthouse, I was ready for a casual ride on my motorcycle to the magnificent and enigmatic Magnetic Hill. Magnetic Hill is a hill located not too far from the city of Leh. It has been strong enough to pull the cars uphill and force the passing aircrafts to increase their altitude in order to escape the magnetic interference. There are some who say that "it is purely an optical effect, which is created by the layout of the surroundings" (gconnect.in, 2009). The argument on what is true and the fact is always a good point of an argument but besides that, it has its own magical beauty. If you place the vehicle in the designated spot and turn the engine off you will soon notice that the vehicle is moving uphill at a good speed. Besides the scientific reasons it surely is a different place to be and enjoy the natural phenomena.

The location enticed me to click some amazing pictures, which did not require much of a focus and framing. While I was enjoying the place clicking pictures, I met a female from Russia who had been travelling in a car and stopped at the magnetic hill to enjoy the rare phenomena. While she was there seeing and enjoying everything I could not help but approach her to click a couple of shots for me with my motorcycle. After a few good shots, we happen to strike a conversation on where I was from and how did I come here and so on. She went speechless on what I had been through so far and felt excited meeting me. I could see the level of excitement she had when she asked her husband to click a few pictures with me and my motorcycle. It feels great when you are highly appreciated for all the effort and dedication you have put into something. I have never experienced something like this before and I was happy and proud about it. With a sweet goodbye and best wishes for my days to come, they were off for their journey. I did bid a final good bye to them and the Magnetic hill.

My next destination was a holy place, which is famous in its own way. It was the 'Patthar Sahib Gurudwara'. Though I am not a Sikh I desperately wanted to visit this very Gurudwara, seek the blessings of the almighty, and thank him for everything I have. I have always seen God in pictures and mythological books but I have never seen an actual silhouette of the almighty. No one has a fair idea about how big the Gods looked but when you actually see this very silhouette it is beyond imagination. With a deep and interesting history behind the very Gurudwara I went blank when I read the story behind the very place.

Picture 1: The magnificent Magnetic hill.
Picture 2: It was peaceful and magical.
Picture 3: Clicked by the woman from Russia.
Picture 4: The Patthar Sahib Gurudwara.
Picture 5: The hill opposite to the Gurudwara.
Picture 6: The stone which turned into a wax ball and touched Guruji.
Picture 7: The food at the Gurudwara was simple, satisfying and more than delicious.
Picture 8: At the Hall of Fame.

The story goes as

'Many years back there lived a Demon on one of the hills situated opposite to where the present Gurudwara is. He always used to kill people and eat them because of which the people in the village were unhappy and sad about it. While Guruji was on his way from Tibet, he stopped at this very place after listening to what had been happening to them. Guruji was taken aback listening to what the villagers have been suffering with and decided to stay back and help them. While Guruji decided to stay back, the Demon was not happy and finally planned to kill Guruji. One day while Guruji was in his prayers the Demon took the advantage of the very moment and rolled a huge boulder towards Guruji. The Demon felt great doing that and happy about the fact that he would not have to face this very holy saint again but what happened when the huge boulder touched Guruji was truly magical. The moment that rolling boulder touched Guruji it turned into a huge ball of wax. Guruji was unknown about this very fact that he had a huge wax boulder behind him. Seeing what the Demon did he felt proud and happy but when he reached the very boulder he was surprised and shocked to see that Guruji was as it is and alive. Irritated and angry the Demon kicked the boulder with his right leg expressing his anger but the moment his leg touched the boulder his leg was into the boulder, which had turned into a ball of wax.

69

After all what had happened the Demon realised that he made a big mistake trying to kill a saint. To set free from the rock he begged Guruji while on his knees to free him. Guruji opened his eyes and guided him to leave what he has been doing which has made him evil and be a people lover and help the community and serve them to the best.'

Looking at that very boulder which turned into a wax and touched Guruji it was more than enough to make me realise that I had touched God. It felt great and so lucky to have this very opportunity. After a good time in the prayer room, I enjoyed the Prasadam, which was a proper lunch in the Gurudwara. It tasted so pure, enjoyable and super satisfying. I was happy that I finally visited the place, which the rest of my friends were not too much interested.

The next stop was the Hall of fame - a place dedicated to army and the winning events in the history of the Indian army. I witnessed some of the martyrs who have lost their lives so that we can be at peace today. Seeing the place, it felt great and proud to be an Indian. It was a worthy experience seeing what goes into making any mission successful and how does the Indian Army survive in the temperature as low as -50 degree Celsius.

I was happy to spend this very day in visiting places which are not so popular but do hold a lot of significance. I felt happy and lucky that I had this very opportunity to spend my day well. By the time, I reached the guesthouse my friends too had reached and I could see them tired, exhausted and a bit hungry while I was energised, charged and relaxed. Listening to what I had missed was pretty much ok for what I had done in those two days was worth cherishing for my own self and satisfaction and I was happy about it.

Distance covered
Kilometres clocked: 50.5

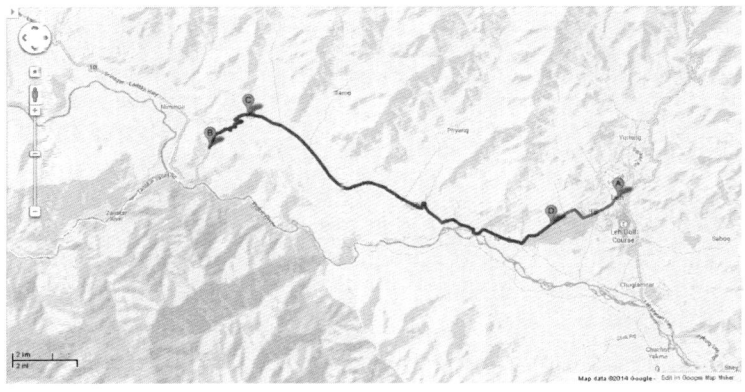

Route map (Source: googlemaps.com)

A to B – Leh city to Magnetic Hill
B to C – Magnetic Hill to Patthar Sahib Gurudwara
C to D – Patthar Sahib Gurudwara to Hall of Fame

Chapter 10

LADAKH SAND DUNES & VISITING THE LORD

After a great day visiting the holy Gurudwara and the magnificent Magnetic Hill it was time now to visit the northern most point of India and to a destination which is known for its Sand dunes and double humped camels. After a great two days of a relaxation, it was time now to travel a bit far but looking at my friends exhaustive faces it seemed more than impossible to ride. After a good thought over everything including the route, we mutually agreed on driving down in our car to Nubra Valley and Hunder sand dunes. With a good two days of a ride to Pangong Tso Lake and back, they looked more than tired to me. I felt a bit eased out for I did have a good time and was lucky to have the much-needed rest against the constant travelling to what they have been doing so far.

With the break of dawn, we were finally off to the valley and enjoying the comfort of a car and enjoying the beauty without any riding gears and thump of a motorcycle. As we had nothing to do besides sharing the experiences we had I did enjoy the pictures they had clicked and felt great listening to the experiences they had. While I was enjoying the pictures, the ball did roll on my court when they asked about what I did when they were gone. To which I did share my pictures, which were more than explanatory. Besides the pictures, I did share my experiences on food, people and exploring the city of Leh on foot. It did not go well with them for they just managed to see one popular lake for I had a chance to see more than one less known destination with enough time to rest and enjoy the nature. While still sharing the experience I could see that the road to the valley did get narrower and narrower and it was not long when I noticed a strange bolder which was flat and had something written on it. It was only after a while I could read and capture a very beautiful advertisement and a word of advice on that very stone. I would not call it an advertisement but more of a milestone written in a different way. It was all about the next point where we could hit the brakes and have some food. It was all about the 'Highest cafeteria in the World'. Looking at the very simple yet different looking structure it felt great being on one of the most notable point in the world. Besides the highest cafeteria in the world, we were also at a point, which is also the Highest Motorable point in the world-the Khardungla Pass.

It was super cold and windy but the excitement and energy felt to be at a place of this cadre it felt more than great. After clicking a few pictures, I did climb on a small stupa opposite to the Cafeteria. It looked so different and of a great importance with the number of colourful prayer flags, I could see. I could not resist myself but to go ahead and explore the less explored. The stupa was small but looked great. The beauty around was no less than what can be portrayed as heaven with clouds around and cold wind running through your hair it was an experience in itself which again my friends were not too interested in. While I was enjoying the beauty of the place and trying to click some of the best shots I can I meet Evabreta the woman from Norway. She was all alone exploring the place just like me. I could not resist but ask her if she could click my picture out there with the prayer flags and near the Stupa. She was more than willing to do that and I helped her doing the same. It was truly magical to be connected to someone you do not know anything about.

We happen to talk about the place and its beauty followed by where she was from. She felt more than normal in spite of the cold, windy weather. It felt great talking to her and clicking a few pictures with her. It was a special moment meeting someone from a different part of the world. We did spend a good time out there in between the prayer flags. It was simply great and something irreplaceable.

While walking down the hill we casually talked about what all destination we have managed to cover and what little is left of it. I was surprised to know that she had the same route and was heading to Nubra Valley too. With an instant laughter on the coincidence, we reached the bottom of the hill followed by a warm hug. She was on her way to her car and with her friends. It was hardly a few moments we had spent together but it was more than enjoyable for me and special too for it is never easy meeting someone in this very memorable place. She would always be special even though I do not know her or for that matter do not even know her full name.

While walking towards the cafeteria my friends did notice everything and started teasing me on whom I was with and what was that all about. I had no wish to spill the beans but to frame a plot satisfactory to them and decent on my end. They did not believe me initially and did ask me every possible question but all thanks to my quick thought I managed it well and made them realise that what I mentioned was the Truth. There are some things you cherish and share it but there are some you keep it special and enjoy it yourself I wanted this to be the latter kind.

After a good bowl of noodles and a black tea, it felt great and energetic too. It was time now to move towards the valley. With everyone, more than charged up we started with a good energy but it was not long when we see a boulder toppling down the hill in front of us. The car halted with a loud screech and a jerk enough to lift us up from the seats. We could not move an inch from the seat nor was my friend willing to take the car further. It was only after a while that I got down with a friend of mine to see what could be the possible scenario. I was a bit shocked to see the way small stones rolled down the very hill. It felt dangerous even standing and seeing that. We had no choice but to wait there until the process slowed down and wait for the road service to reach the spot and clear the road from the boulder. Luckily, they arrived soon and began pushing the boulder with the rod. I could not see them doing alone and started helping them push the boulder to the side. It was not easy moving that gigantic piece of rock until the corner of the road. It was only after a good half an hour of the pushing exercise we had managed to clear the road.

The road was open and free to move forward. With a loud thank you and a good-bye, we moved forward. It felt relieved sitting back in the car and recovering from the heavy breath. It was not easy pushing the boulder in this very climate, which has less oxygen and cold winds on your face.

After a smooth journey towards the Valley, I did have a good nap. I could feel the weather changing from a bit cold to now a bit warmer though it was not sunny it felt a bit different. When I woke up, I was surprised to see the deserted flat lands with no trees around and a feel of desert. It felt a bit warmer and pleasant because of the air conditioner in the car, which helped me sleep, but when I rolled down the window, I could feel the difference. With such a vast difference in the climate it was tough accepting the fact that I was shivering in cold winds an hour back and now I am sweating because of the hot air. I wonder how the people in this region adopt to this vary-

With passing through the deserted land and a few small hills, I did notice a huge statue on one of the hills. With my eyes glued at the statue, I could not wait to see on what that could be. It was after a while that I realised that it is a Lord Buddha statue which looked magnificently huge from the bottom of the hill.

We continued towards the valley and decided to stop by on our return journey. After a long time travelling we were finally seeing the Sand dunes. They looked majestic. I had never seen a sand dune before and so wished to go there and walk on them. After passing through the entry gates to the Hunder village, we had an access road towards the Sand Dunes. While we walked towards them, it felt super hot. For a while, I never thought that we were on such a high altitude and on the northern part of India. It felt like the desert in the state of Rajasthan. They truly were beautiful and felt great to be on them. After a few yards of walking around, I did notice that there were a few trees just like the ones in the tropical region followed by a small stream of water passing by the trees. I had never seen this very scenario and heard of it too. For what I had known so far, it was just the sand dunes, which you see in the desert, and it is tough to find water on them but this was very different. It felt cooler when you are closer the stream and pleasant while you are near the woods. I had no words to express this magical change in the nature in such a short distance. It purely was beyond imagination.

Picture 1: One of the most amazing captions I have ever seen on the road.
Picture 2: It is priceless to be here and experience the weather and place filled with prayer flags.
Picture 3: The magnificent view of the Lord Buddha Statue.
Picture 4: The amazing Ladakh Sand Dunes.
Picture 5: The only place where I could see the Sand Dunes with the water stream flowing by with some trees.

I decided to enjoy the beauty and click as many pictures as I could. It was after a while we noticed some camels. They looked amazing and were not the ones we saw regularly. They were the double humped camels. The camel owners did offer a ride on them in the sand dunes for a small fee but I was not too sure to go ahead with the same and nor were my friends.

We enjoyed seeing them and walked back to the car. I could feel the difference in temperature with the heat outside and the temperature inside the car. With a bit of a relaxing we moved on towards Diskit Monastery.

With the hot weather outside, we could not help but turn up the air conditioner and feel comfortable while we approached the huge statue. It looks beautiful from kilo metres away. I wondered how tall the statue would be when you are under it. After driving a few kilometres, we diverted the route towards the hill and reached the gates to the Diskit Monastery. It looked beautiful.

The Lord Buddha statue was on the left and the monastery on the right on another hill. I wonder how the monks would be surviving in a place so remote and without any connectivity. It feels great being in such a peaceful location but being a part of this place for months is not easy. Visiting the gigantic statue, I was awestruck the way it shone in sun and the look it had. I had never seen something like that before. I was awestruck with the beauty and purity it had. It felt as if I was next to the actual Lord and enjoying his company. With the peaceful atmosphere and a bit pleasant than the sand dunes in Hunder I did take some time to enjoy the place and click some pictures but unfortunately in a place like this more is less when it comes to spending the time. We had to reach Leh before it gets dark and so we started again.

After driving for a few kilometres, we did notice a long queue on the road full of cars, motorcycles and a couple of trucks too. We had no clue on what could that be before we could reach the place and witness it with our own eyes. We quickly merged into the queue.

A few of my friends did go to the place where everyone had gathered just to see on what the problem could be. It was only after a good half an hour that we realised that a truck carrying a bulldozer had stopped on one of the turns and would not be able to move forward until the problem is fixed. Because of the narrow road at the very spot, it was difficult to drive next to it. While we reached the location, some of the drivers had already started building a narrow stone road kind of a thing, which is strong enough to support, and empty car and pass that turn. It was after a good teamwork and extensive effort to broaden the road we could go ahead. The extended road was prepared with the rocks stacked in a way, which would give it a similar height to the tar road, and strong enough to let the cars go ahead on top of it. It was no easy task but the moment first vehicle passed by it was easy for the rest for everyone knew how the best he or she could go ahead passing that obstacle.

With every such experience we had so far, it felt tough in the beginning but we did manage it well and moved forward to the next level. Besides the adventure and adrenaline rush it is also the patience and endurance to face the situation, which matters. I have been lucky enough to have an easy fix and smooth ride so far and I am happy about it. Besides every glitch we had so far, we are yet to face something more interesting and intense when we start riding again tomorrow for Manali. It would be one hell of a ride back to the place from where we started.

The epic journey to these beautiful mountains and the mesmerizing city of Leh has come to an end. Though everyone wished to go back home but no one wanted to 'ride' back to Manali. I was prepared for it and was not too exhausted like my friends were and so had an added advantage of being in the city and enjoying the nearby less known locations than visiting the Pangong Tso Lake. It is necessary to have adequate rest in order to enjoy the trip and not have the painful experience. With everyone preparing themselves and the motorcycles for the ride tomorrow the point of discussion diverted to where can we have our dinner.

With the last day in this beautiful city of Leh everyone decided to go ahead with a special place and enjoy the sumptuous food. We finally zeroed in on a place called La Pizzeria. It looked amazing to see different open tents with the tables in them for a great dining experience. We finalised on a big tent which had two tables and there were some who were already inside enjoying their food. It felt great sitting so far and hope that the experience with food would be great too. While we were talking about the plan for the next day there was an unrecognised voice from the other tables which said something.

Picture 1: Double-Humped camel (Photo courtesy: Sumit Parlikar, fellow rider).
Picture 2: Gate to the Diskit Monastery.
Picture 3: The Diskit Monastery.
Picture 4: The Lord Buddha Temple opposite to the Monastery.
Picture 5: The Lord.
Picture 6: Teamwork on broadening the road.
Picture 7: Every stone is stacked carefully to avoid any errors.

In a polite form I asked them if they said something to which he replied in our mother tongue 'Gujarati'. Gujarati's are known for their nature no matter where they are in the world and especially when it comes to sharing the same taste and situations makes them best of the buddies. It was no different out here too and while interacting about where we were from and where I did my schooling from I was enlightened to the fact that two of my friends stay in the same very colony where two of those guys on the next table stayed. While interacting a bit on my school and my friends those two guys knew a lot about them. It feels great and more connected when you have some common connections out of the blue. I never had imagined that I would come across someone who would know many of my friends from my school. I was delighted and happy. While I swiftly moved my attention to the third guy who looked a bit healthier and taller than the other two. I asked him if he was from Gujarat too to which he swiftly answered 'I am from Mumbai and I work for one of the famous five star hotels'. While he mentioned about his workplace I have a friend who works in the same place too and to my surprise and a bit of a shock he knew him. I could not be more surprised when I had some or the other connection all the three of them who I meet out of nowhere. It felt great and I was delighted to the fact that we had some known company but sadly at the end of the trip.

After discussing on what all we did and what our plan was it felt a bit strange to know that they were done with the trip too and would be leaving for Manali. I do not know what to call this- a strange coincidence or a planned destiny? Whatever it was, it surely made me happy. After a quick dinner and sharing all the possible experiences it was time now to head back to the guest house and take the much needed rest for it is going to be a tiring day ahead of us tomorrow. While riding back to the guest house I did take a long route enjoying the quiet city and how enjoyable some of these days were.

Distance covered
Kilometers clocked: 140

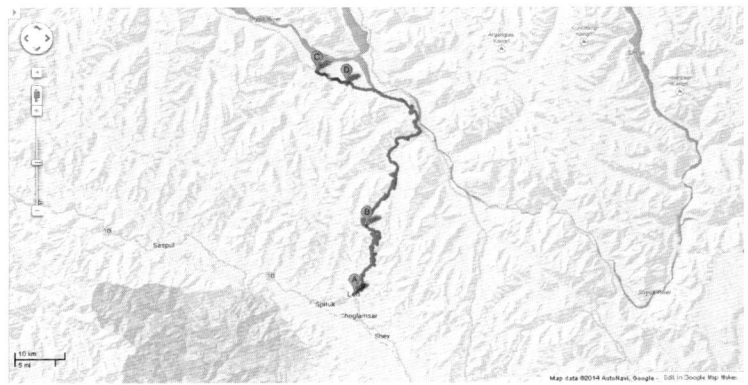

Route map (Source: googlemaps.com)

A to B – Guest house to Khardung La Pass
B to C – Khardung La Pass to Hunder Sand Dunes
C to D – Hunder Sand Dunes to Diskit Monastery

Chapter 11

BACK TO WHERE
WE STARTED FROM

With an early morning and a final check already done with the baggage and the motorcycle it felt great to gear up again for one of the most treacherous ride of our journey. 5 am in the morning when I receive a call from our new company who too were riding back to Manali with us. They were ready and would be meeting us at the pre-decided spot in some time. It felt great that we would have some company and I guess they would be feeling the same as well. With a silent kick and a sudden thump bringing the motorcycle to life we escalated towards the meeting point. A final check on the fuel, tyre pressure and our own self we were ready to go.

A lot had changed from as we leave Leh compared to when we reached. No one throttled hard and zoomed ahead, everyone followed a common rule about riding with a discipline, which I guess lacked when we rode to Leh. I was happy that it has been turning up the way it was supposed to be. With a steady pace and cherishing all those moments I had with the city I felt bad seeing the place passing by. I would surely be missing the city for I connected well and felt great being a part of it. Enjoying the sweet memories, it felt great but I was also to ride on those tough and treacherous passes. I hated riding on our journey to Leh but it felt great and confident to ride again on them maybe because of the familiarity with the motorcycle I was riding and a good awareness of the road

I would have to go through. I was more confident and active than before.

Besides the confident ride it was some of the patches, which I wanted to be super careful about, and one of them was the Gata Loops- a twenty hairpin bends loop. The location offers great panoramic view but it is one of those places where no one stops without a reason. A few bends on to the loops and we spotted a spot, which was frankly an eyesore in the middle of this pristine landscape. A small temple like structure with so many bottles around which initially looked as a trash while we were heading to Leh but it actually was an offering at the temple like structure.

The story goes as

Many years ago, a truck broke down on the same bend. The driver, aware of the cargo he was carrying, asked the cleaner to stay back with the truck while he walked to the nearest village to get some help. Off he went, trudging the forty kilometres of mountain roads that separated him from inhabitation.

When he reached the spot, he could not find any help in sight. He could clearly see that a storm on another pass had closed the road, there were no mechanics found in the tiny village and, even as the driver waited, the weather closed in. The driver was in the village stranded for over a week before a mechanic and a vehicle came by. By the time they reached the truck, they found the cleaner dead, felled by exposure and thirst, high on the bone-dry mountainside. Rather than carrying a decomposing body home, the rescuers buried the cleaner close by.

Things started happening a few months later when the travellers stopping on the loops started meeting a man who begged them piteously for water. People who refused were soon writhing with mountain sickness, and some even died of it.

Those who obliged, though, saw the bottles they offered drop through the man's hands, while he kept pleading for water. Terror struck the region as the news about this very incident spread the nearby and subsided only when the locals had set up a memorial at the site and made offerings of water to placate the ghost. (vinoddsa, 2011)

It was a smooth ride until Pang where we had our lunch and some much-needed rest. Though the loops were after Sarchu- the spot where we would be doing our night halt I was more than cautious about the whole incident and everything which passed by.

Passing the extra dry patch after pang we could finally see some greenery and just when I could see some water flowing I came across a huge stream. I had to cross through with great care, caution and focus on what lies beneath that clear water. With a steady pace and a clear eye in the stream, it felt good passing that stream without much of an effort. I was more than confident and felt more like a pro after riding in so much of a rough and rugged terrain.

Picture 1: Gata Loops Start Point (Picture courtesy: Sumit Parlikar, fellow rider).
Picture 2: Gata Loops End Point (Picture courtesy: Sumit Parlikar, fellow rider).
Picture 3: The actual location where the incident happened many years ago (Picture Courtesy: Sumit Parlikar, fellow rider).
Picture 4: The Gata Loops (Picture Courtesy: Sumit Parlikar, fellow rider).
Picture 5: As viewed on the Google maps.
Picture 6: It feels great to have the potatoes cooked in spices with some Indian bread. A much-needed simple but special meal.
Picture 7: It was one of the best nights.

I never wanted to be over confident but never wanted to ride with less confidence and doubt about any terrain I am on.

With a swift and slow ride we reached the much awaited check post where we had to produce our ID's, get the clearance and wait for the fellow riders who were soon to be followed. The check post is set up with an intention to keep a close check on the vehicles, which pass by and on the same number of vehicles which has initially passed by do cross the check post again and make an exit from that very check post. Failing to do so the check post would contact the other posts, inquire about the missing vehicle, and call for a search party between the locations where the vehicle is not re-registered.

After all the necessary formalities, we were on our way to accommodation tents. However, Sarchu is one of the famous spot in between Manali to Leh but it does not have any major accommodation facilities besides the tents in amazing flat plains in between the mountains. The tents looked big and spacious with attached toilet and a bathing area. It was something I had never seen before and above all, they looked very comfortable, clean and spacious. While we stayed in a different location while riding to Leh it was recommended by three of our new friends who had initially stayed here and do suggest that the food offered here tastes amazing.

It felt great to see a huge tent, which was a designated dining tent with a good number of chairs and tables, and above all, it had some things, which I never thought that I would be seeing here- a good set of speakers and disco lights.

We were the only people who were staying back in those tents for the night so in a way we owned the place and would not be a problem to listen to some music and feel like we are in the club.

Looking at the place my friends decided to make it memorable with some alcohol and a lot of dancing. Everyone gathered in and danced to some of the known tunes while enjoying some Rum and Coke. It was one of the best nights one could think of especially in this very terrain where there was no humanity around for many kilometres away. It felt great, special, and above all pain free after a long ride during the day. After a good clubbing experience, it was time now to have some sumptuous dinner and end the day. While heading to bed I did cherish the moments I had so far experienced and with a gentle smile on my face I was off to sleep.

Distance covered
Kilometers clocked: 237

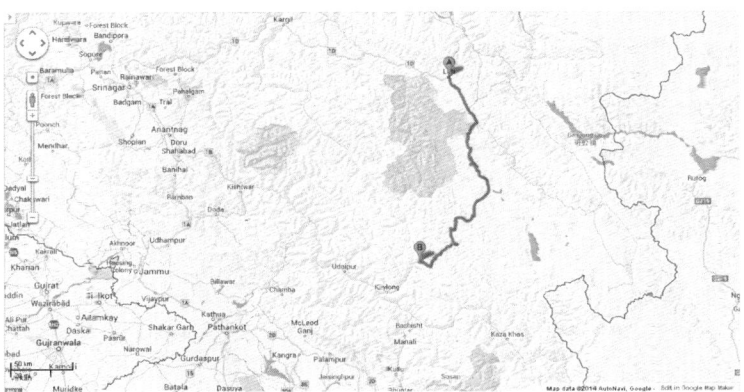

Route map (Source: googlemaps.com)

Chapter 12

THE LONGEST DAY OF MY LIFE

With a cold breeze blowing through the tents and waking me up with a great morning it was the day when I would finish the last leg of the journey. Rough roads and streams with no life around was a passé which holds a great memory in my heart. With a good sound sleep I had it felt great being ready for the last day riding in between these beautiful passes and land of pure mysteries. Sipping on some black tea which I never drink and munching on some 'Aloo Parantha' whole wheat Indian flat bread made with Aloo or potatoes. Besides potatoes it can be made with various stuffing's and is a staple bread in Northern India (manjulakitchen.com, 2009) it felt great and charged up to ride again.

While I was up early and ready to go it was my friends who were in their own pace but did seem to be excited about reaching Manali. In the meanwhile I checked up my motorcycle and refueled it while the rest refueled their stomach. After brief information about the road ahead from the person in-charge for the tents we made a swift move towards Manali. Everyone seemed more than enthusiastic to reach the final destination and enjoy the much needed comfort of the hotel and a good hot shower.

Everything seemed fine as we flagged off riding from our accommodation tents towards Manali when suddenly our lead rider stopped on one of the key hair pin turns after a shallow stream. While everyone gathered up I was last to ride in the pact and noticed everyone gathering up and noticing something in the rear wheels. While I made an occasional glance at the halted group I could not wait to reach there soon and know what went wrong. It was after a good fifteen-twenty minutes I reached the hair pin turn and noticed that one of the motorcycles had a flat tyre. I checked on the situation but it was nothing more we could do besides loosening the shaft bolts and seek some help from the riders or drivers passing by for a key tool which we unfortunately did not have it with us.

While eagerly waiting for people to pass by my friend noticed a solo rider with a good amount of luggage on his luggage racks. While we all waited for him my eyes eagerly followed his movements and there was a time when I could not see him anymore. With an anticipated look and waiting to see him ride through that much unseen patch I could not resist but ride down to that very location and see where he was. While I rode down to see where that solo rider was I had some of the most dangerous thoughts in my mind and vanished only when I saw him getting up in between the stream and his motorcycle on his right leg. As I was riding down with my friend we wasted no time and helped him get off the motorcycle and walk out of the stream while my friend dragged the motorcycle out of the stream.

The rider looked more than scared and a bit numb but felt better when we offered him some warm water and some sweets. He was all wet under his waist and that made him shiver to the core for it is the ice water stream which passes by the same very place. It was after a while he asked us on how we spotted him and why were we all waiting at this very unusual spot. A bit of a clear view of the motorcycle gave him a fair idea about the reason why we were waiting at that very usual spot.

Looking at the motorcycle he smiled and asked us if he could be of any help to us. While we asked him for a particular tool he wasted no time and unpacked his tool kit from his heavy luggage and gave everything to us. We finally had the tool and managed to open up the tyre and remove the tyre tube and replace it with the new one for it would be tough to locate the puncture in the tube and repair it.

While the new tube was being replaced the American solo rider could not see us doing everything and gave us a helping hand changing the tube and pumping some air.

While he pumped for a while he could not hold his breath because of the climate and had to pass it on to others who can continue inflating the repaired tyre. While everyone took a turn one by one everyone was more than interactive with Kevin as he mentioned his name is. While he narrated on where all he had been to and where he wishes to go everyone was more than numb about his plan and went speechless knowing the fact that he left his white collar job, divorced his wife, sold off his assets and off he came in between these vary valleys to know himself and experience the raw nature. Every word he said felt more than pure and very much from his heart to which I had no thoughts to express. I was not able to think of anything which I could think of asking him besides which route he wishes to follow.

Picture 1: That was a good Morning with a Black Tea.
Picture 2: It is mandatory to carry some fuel with you while riding on this route.
Picture 3: Our accommodation for the night.
Picture 4: A final picture before we leave back for Manali.
Picture 5: A flat tyre in this region is no less than a nightmare.

With a calm and composed voice he asked us about what all experiences we had so far to which a couple of us did mention a few of what we had experienced so far which sounded more of bits compared to what he had been experiencing being a solo rider. As people continued to take turns in pumping more and more air in the tyre through the manual bicycle pump it became more and more difficult as everyone was tired by now after a good two hours of non-stop pumping.

Kevin looked more than ready to ride again. We could not stop him but gave him his tool box and with a simple caring smile and a brief good bye wave he moved forward.

By now we had managed to fix the tyre with a new tube and have been pumping as much air as possible though failing to reach the tyre pressure it should be at. This made all of us more than tired by now which left us with no choice but to wait for any vehicles which passed by and ask about an 'Puncture shop' available if any in a nearby villages.

Picture 1: A helping hand from Kevin.
Picture 2: To the puncture shop.
Picture 3: It does not look like a puncture shop but it actually is one.
Picture 4: A not so comfortable nap while waiting for my fellow riders.
Picture 5: Believe it or not but this is what took our Eight hours (Photo Courtesy: Sumit Parlikar, fellow rider).
Picture 6: With a slow but steady pace we pranced forward (Photo Courtesy: Sumit Parlikar, fellow rider).
Picture 7: A short break after Darcha just for this picture was much needed (Photo Courtesy: Sumit Parlikar, fellow rider).

After a good few vehicles which were helpless to some of our questions a tempo driver helped us out with a puncture shop directions which did not seem too far. Upon knowing the precise direction and distance which has to be measured counting the number of hills passed by my friend left with the semi-fixed tyre.

A few minutes turned into an hour and eventually into a few hours when everyone was more than concerned about where he could possibly be taking so much of time. No one could think of anything safe and better with every possible worst scenarios playing up in the head it made us think worst. I finally made a move with my friend in our SUV driving towards the puncture shop as directed by the tempo driver. While driving to the destination we could not think of anything or talk to each other thinking about all the possible worst case scenarios and scared about the fact that we might find him somewhere.

Upon reaching the puncture shop after a good half an hour of a drive we were at ease to find his motorcycle and him fixing the tyre while the puncture shop fellow looked on. Upon asking him why he was doing everything while the other guy directing him we were enlightened with a strange fact.

If at all you have a flat tyre in between Manali and Leh it would be your responsibility to dismantle the tyre from the vehicle and remove the tube after which the puncture guy would fix the problem and give it back to you to set the tube in the tyre and give it back to him to inflate the tyre. It was strange and a bit rude but felt completely justifiable when we were made aware of the very reason. As the locations between Manali and Leh is on high altitude it becomes difficult to carry on a stringent and tiring activity specially when it involves dismantling the tyres and tubes and refitting them it becomes very difficult to carry the whole process smoothly and that too with limited ration and facilities.

I could totally relate to the situation and its intensity and carried on without any further questions. After a while everything was sorted and just about the time when we planned to go back to the puncture location there was a sudden rainfall. It went on for a good one hour which left us with no choice but to wait for it to stop and resume the journey back to the hairpin turn. As we waited for the rains to stop the fellow riders present on the hair pin with their respective motorcycles experienced the sudden hail storm which left them with no choice but to leave the single wheeled motorcycle behind and ride to one of the nearby check post in order to have some protection from the hailstorm. While leaving from the location they did managed to make a huge arrow pointing their whereabouts towards the nearby check post.

On our end everything seemed fine after a good one hour and we decided to roll. As the puncture shop was after 'Zingzingbar' me and my friend who had come down in the SUV decided to stay back at the tents thinking it would be difficult to turn the car at the hair pin turn. We mutually agreed to which my friend moved on with the tyre tied on the motorcycle. After a quick nap and a lot of waiting we were more than worried about where everyone would be. With no communication available it was difficult to understand what could have been the problem. With no choice left we had to wait and watch and let the weird dangerous thoughts roll our heads till the time we do not see their safe faces in front of us. It was after a good three hours the rest of the clan arrived at the tent.

I could see them shivering but uncontrollable to the bad thoughts about them we had some heated arguments about why they took so long in fixing things up and come down to the tent. After a good elaborative story from both the ends it was a bit cool. It was definitely one of the most unpleasant moments where you are more than unsure of how would your fellow riders being.

With everything in place and intact we had spent a good eight hours to be back on track and ride to Manali. With everything clear and fine we were back on track towards Manali leaving behind Zingzingbar.

With the roads improving every few miles I could see the darkness enveloping the skies driving the time to dusk and leading to darkness. With a good pace and no stop ride we managed to reach Darcha the final check post on our way to Manali. After the clearance I chose to ride on while others made a brief halt for their regular smoke. While I passed by the check post and climbed up one of the bad hairpins I could feel myself loosing the balance due to a bit of a sharp turn I took on my motorcycle leading to a point where I could not rev up my motorcycle due to some reason and before it could get worst I left the motorcycle and jumped on the side while my motorcycle fell on the hair pin turn. I could not do anything but stare at my motorcycle which was lying on the road. It was within no time that some of the people gathered and helped me lift my motorcycle and drag it to the side and asked me if I was ok and needed any help too. I was fine but a bit lost mentally maybe because of the ride fatigue. I fired up the engine and thanked everyone who helped and moved on. It was no less than a wakeup call for I would not want another crash and go home with a severe injury or bruises.

I was back on track and smooth with the pace but not enough to reach Kaylong before it turned a bit dark. My fellow riders who were busy smoking had rushed a bit and now riding together with me making me the lead rider. After an hour or so we reached Kaylong and it was already getting darker and darker which means we would either have to go back to the next village called Jispa for an overnight stay or continue riding on Rohtang Pass and reach Manali whenever possible.

With no one eager to turning back from Kaylong we decided to be swift and started riding towards Rohtang Pass. It was around 7 pm in the evening and it was dark by the time we started riding on Rohtang pass which means we have just our headlights to guide us and our feet to give us a surely of a firm land beneath us. With every turn passing by I tried to recall on the locations where we had the mud slush for we would have to be more than careful passing that patch for it is narrower than the rest of the road and might stop the vehicle due to excessive mud. I could feel the slush as my handlebar moved left and right without my guidance which left me with no choice but to guide my motorcycle with my legs and firm steering movements which would help me ride straight.

After a good four hours of struggling we had managed to reach the summit and a bit of a smooth road which clearly indicated that we were on the summit and now it was the real challenge to ride in the mud slush with no lights and no guidance from anyone besides your heart and your gut feeling. I took a deep breath while I moved forward and entered the mud slush patch which as far as I remember was a bit easy. My body ached to the core but I had no choice but to ride on to those tiny lights downhill where the beautiful town of Manali was. Slow and steady every one followed me while I followed my heart and the firmness my legs indicated on. With no stops and no looking sideways in the darkness I moved on. It was after a good four hours of treacherous, nerve wracking and tiring ride in the dark and on the mud slush we managed to ride on a tar road which leads to Manali. I kept the same pace until I reached Manali. I could see my friends and fellow riders passing by with joy and happiness.

We had finally made it to Manali and that we take it easy and find a place to stay and eat. It was past midnight that we had reached and it would be a bit difficult to find some food and maybe an accommodation too but all thanks to the local police we managed to find both and in a reasonable price.

While everyone entered the room and freshened up no one uttered a word. Everyone was among themselves tired, hungry and frustrated to the core doing the last leg. I could now proudly say that I made it and made it well. With a quiet dinner which everyone had, no one bothered to change besides removing their riding gears and shoes and dozed off in no time. With a good sense of achievement but teary eyes I dozed off remembering about how long and tiring a day could possibly be.

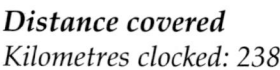

Distance covered
Kilometres clocked: 238

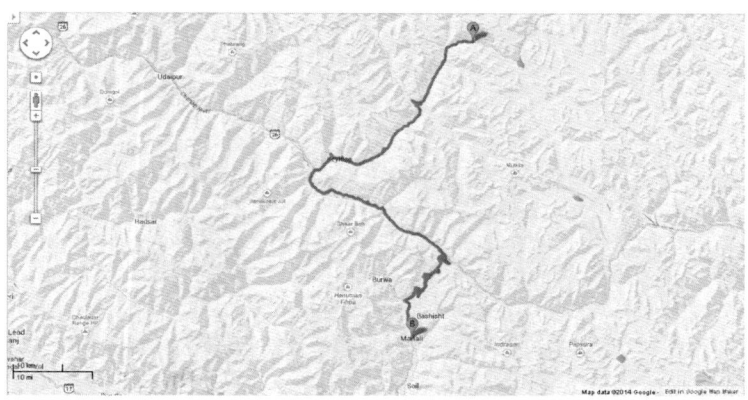

Route map (Source: googlemaps.com)

FAQs

? Is there a particular time of the year you can plan a trip to Leh?

The city of Leh has its season and peak time from the month of May to July. It would be ideal time to do this very trip during the mentioned months to avoid road closures and extremely cold climate. However, there are many who ride in the month of August and September too. If you are an amateur rider or someone, who is not used to riding long distance can think of doing this trip in the month of July.

? Can we take any other route besides the Manali-Leh route?

You can choose the Srinagar-Ladakh highway which pass through Kargil and Drass. The route has its own beauty. It would not be as treacherous to ride on compared to Manali-Leh route. The former route would come to around 416 kms, which is a bit shorter compared to Manali-Leh route, which is 474 kms.

? What is the minimum number of days one can plan this trip for?

When it comes to an adventurous trip like this, it is better to have a few buffer days just in case you wish to visit a few less known locations or enjoy the stay in any of the places in and around Leh. It would be better to plan a trip no less than 15 days counting from the day you reach Manali.

 Which is the best motorcycle to ride on this terrain?

It is better to have a motorcycle that is comfortable to ride on, and strong enough to handle the rough terrain but to go into specifics it is better to ride on a Royal Enfield. It has a bigger engine and heavier than the rest of the motorcycles available in the Indian automobile market. Besides the powerful engine, it also has a sturdy frame and a good road clearance, which is quintessential while crossing the streams. Besides the Royal Enfield, many do recommend the Hero Karizma a roadster kind of a motorcycle with a bit of a smaller engine compared to the Enfield.

 How do you fix the serious breakdowns in this region?

Before planning this very trip, it is necessary to prepare yourself and know the basics about fixing the motorcycle you would be riding on. The basic knowledge would also give you a brief idea about the kind of spares you would need to take along with you while on the trip. Planning this trip without a proper back up plan would be a pure planning for failure.

I have a problem breathing in high altitude. Can I think about doing this trip?

Yes, you can. Before you plan to go on this very trip it is essential to keep yourself fit and follow the rigorous training plan mentioned in the beginning of the book. Besides keeping fit it is necessary to do a lot of breathing exercises. While riding on the trip it is necessary to be hydrated and energised at all times as you would not realise the falling sugar level and dehydration but feel a mild headache which is nothing but a signal from your brain about less oxygen. Drinking a good five to six litres of water a few hours would solve this problem. In case of emergency, you can always stop at the any army camp where you receive the necessary medications and treatments.

 I wish to do this very trip but I do not own a motorcycle?

You can still do this very trip by hiring a motorcycle from Manali, Jammu or New Delhi depending on your destination. A Royal Enfield Classic (350 cc) would be available for Rs. 1200-1300 per day with a deposit of Rs. 15-20,000 (prices vary every year). The amount has to be paid in advance with the rental amount for a minimum of ten days. Besides the amount you need to pay it is necessary to have your driving license handy at all times with a good number of photocopies to avoid last minute hassle.

What are the places I can visit to once I reach Leh?

There are many places to visit in and around Leh. It all depends on the number of days you have and your group size. To name a few;
- Sarchu, known for its captivating night sky,
- Khardung La, known to be one of the world's highest motorable roads,
- Nubra valley with a couple of nights in Turtuk,
- and the famous Pangong Tso Lake.

(?) How can I do this trip if I am foreign national?

You can certainly plan and do this very trip. It would be necessary to have the International Driving license, which would help you obtain the motorcycle on rent as well pass through the check posts. It would also be necessary to have all the original Identity proofs along with the photocopies handy just in case an official demands one for himself or herself.

Bibliography

- 30dayfitnesschallenges.com. 30 day arms challenge chart. n.d.
- 60kph.com. Packing for a long ride. 2006.
- chicken.ca. Chicken Thukpa (Himalayan Noodle Soup). 2012.
- gconnect.in. Magnetic Hill Leh-Ladakh-Mystery Explained. 2009.
- http://girevoysportafter40.blogspot.in/. Flexibility in GS. 2008. Leibenluft, J. Drunk and High in Denver. n/a.
- Lindberg.G. How to Do Forearm Exercises. n/a.
- manjulakitchen.com. Faratha (Whole wheat flat bread). 2009.
- McKenzie, Kelvin. Top 5 lower back workouts for men at home. 2012.
- n/a. my health. 2012.
- Nakamura, Most Ven. Gyomyo. Ladakh Shanti Stupa. New Delhi, 2013.
- Rajdhani.co.in. Dal Baati Churma. n.d.
- studentphysicaltherapy.tumblr.com. Physical therapy stuff. 2012.
- travel.india.com. Namgyal Tsemo Gompa. 2013.
- vinoddsa. The Ghost of Gata Loops. 2011.
- Waitley.D. Exciting quotes. n.d.

About the Author

Janak is a 1984 born, MSc and MBA educated from Mumbai, India. He is an avid traveller by choice and a solopreneur by luck. He has clocked many thousands of kilometres on a motorcycle.

It was his journey to the Leh-Ladakh which motivated him to write about his experiences throughout the journey in enjoying the beauty, pain and hardships.

He is passionate about travelling and photography which helps him find a beauty and meaning in this wide busy world.

Email: *janaknmistry@yahoo.com*
Twitter: *www.twitter.com/janaknmistry*
Facebook: *www.facebook.com/janaknmistry*